"I need someone to act as my girlfriend this weekend."

It was Thursday. How was Whitney going to find someone who would go away with a perfect stranger on such short notice? "I wish I could help you, Tanner. At this point I don't know what I can do."

"Well, I do. If you can't find me someone, then you have to come."

What? Was he crazy? Spend a weekend with him? "That's not possible. It's unethical. You're my client."

"One you're expected to keep happy. This weekend is important to my career, just as finding the right woman is. There will be no expectations on my part except for you to be pleasant and act as if we're a couple." His voice was firm and determined, as if he wouldn't accept no for an answer.

Whitney's heart pounded. Was she seriously going to consider it? "You can't just demand that I spend the weekend with you."

If she agreed, she couldn't imagine the weekend being anything but long and miserable. She didn't belong in his social group. She was an outsider. Tanner wanted someone who could make a good impression. He needed someone who could influence. That wasn't her. She was good with people one-on-one, but not as a member of a house party. To run in Tanner's world…

"I'll pick you up at nine in the morning."

"Tanner, I can't do this."

"You can and you will."

Dear Reader,

I never know where a story idea is going to come from. This one literally came from the sky. While I was on a plane and reading the airline magazine I noticed an advertisement for a matchmaker who specialized in helping the busy professional. A spark of an idea was born that became Whitney and Tanner's story. This was a fun one to write, especially when this couple finds out that what they want is right under their noses. The setting isn't bad either— San Francisco and Napa Valley.

I hope you enjoy the journey that Whitney and Tanner take on their way to finding true love. Hearing from my readers is one of my greatest joys. You can contact me at susancarlisle.com.

Happy reading,

Susan

THE SURGEON'S CINDERELLA

———

SUSAN CARLISLE

HARLEQUIN® MEDICAL ROMANCE™

If you purchased this book without a cover you should be aware that this book is stolen property. It was reported as "unsold and destroyed" to the publisher, and neither the author nor the publisher has received any payment for this "stripped book."

Recycling programs
for this product may
not exist in your area.

ISBN-13: 978-0-373-21534-8

The Surgeon's Cinderella

First North American Publication 2017

Copyright © 2017 by Susan Carlisle

All rights reserved. Except for use in any review, the reproduction or utilization of this work in whole or in part in any form by any electronic, mechanical or other means, now known or hereinafter invented, including xerography, photocopying and recording, or in any information storage or retrieval system, is forbidden without the written permission of the publisher, Harlequin Enterprises Limited, 225 Duncan Mill Road, Don Mills, Ontario M3B 3K9, Canada.

This is a work of fiction. Names, characters, places and incidents are either the product of the author's imagination or are used fictitiously, and any resemblance to actual persons, living or dead, business establishments, events or locales is entirely coincidental.

This edition published by arrangement with Harlequin Books S.A.

For questions and comments about the quality of this book, please contact us at CustomerService@Harlequin.com.

® and TM are trademarks of Harlequin Enterprises Limited or its corporate affiliates. Trademarks indicated with ® are registered in the United States Patent and Trademark Office, the Canadian Intellectual Property Office and in other countries.

Printed in U.S.A.

www.Harlequin.com

Books by Susan Carlisle

Harlequin Medical Romance

Summer Brides

White Wedding for a Southern Belle

Midwives On-Call

His Best Friend's Baby

Heart of Mississippi

The Maverick Who Ruled Her Heart
The Doctor Who Made Her Love Again

Married for the Boss's Baby
The Doctor's Sleigh Bell Proposal

Visit the Author Profile page
at Harlequin.com for more titles.

To Eric
Everyone should have a son-in-law like you.

**Praise for
Susan Carlisle**

"Gripping, stirring, and emotionally touching... A perfect medical read!"

—*Goodreads* on
His Best Friend's Baby

"This emotional love story kept me riveted. A truly satisfying, emotional read. Susan Carlisle's work is like that. Check it out, you won't be disappointed."

—*Goodreads* on
NYC Angels: The Wallflower's Secret

CHAPTER ONE

TANNER LOCKE NEEDED a matchmaker's help.

Two days earlier Whitney Thomason's hand had quivered slightly as she'd held the phone. He was certainly a blast from the past. Why would someone like Tanner require her help?

An hour earlier he had texted her that he needed to change their arrangements and asked her to meet him at a small airport outside San Francisco. As the owner of Professional Matchmaking, Whitney had made concessions for clients on more than one occasion, but this was the first time she'd been asked to meet one at an airport at dusk.

Tanner had said something had come up and that he couldn't join her at her office. He would appreciate her meeting him at the airport. If she hadn't been familiar with his status in the community she wouldn't have considered such a plan. She wasn't acquainted with the small airport but had agreed to do as he'd requested.

Having *the* Dr. Tanner Locke's name on her client list would be good for business. Even though it was unethical to publicize his name, she could say that an eminent doctor in the city had used her services. Who knew? He might even send her referrals. Either of those would make it worth her drive to meet him.

As the "big man on campus" when they'd been at Berkeley, all the girls had had a crush on Tanner, including herself. But she hadn't been his style. He had been into thin, blonde, preppy sorority girls while she had been the heavy, dark-haired, mousy nobody. At least she already knew his type.

In the past couple of years she'd seen Tanner's name in the news a few times. He was an up-and-coming surgeon in the heart transplant field. So why did someone as good-looking and eligible as Tanner need her help in finding a mate?

Whitney chuckled drily. For the same reasons her other clients did. They didn't have the time or energy to weed out the unsuitable. She handled the nitty-gritty work of finding people with similar backgrounds so they only connected with the people most appropriate for them. It was a one-and-done process.

She rolled through the gate of the airfield minutes before she was due to meet Tanner. Would he recognize her? Why should he? She'd just been one of those people who had been a filler in a couple of his classes. Plus she'd changed a great deal since then. At least on the outside. She'd lost fifty pounds. She'd long outgrown having a crush on Tanner. Heavens, she didn't even really know him.

Pulling into a parking spot in the lot next to a red single-story, cement-block building, she turned off the engine. A gleaming white jet sat on the tarmac in front of the terminal. There were a couple of men working around it. Was Tanner going somewhere? Probably off to Hawaii for the weekend.

Normally Whitney liked to have her initial interview in a neutral and laid-back place. A local café, the park. Out of the client's high-pressure work world so that they were more relaxed, less distracted. She found that even though people's favorite subject was themselves, when it came to their personal life they weren't as forthcoming. Men tended toward telling about half of what she needed to know. The more successful her client was, the more insecure or demanding or both they were about their choices for mates.

At the sound of an ambulance siren, she glanced into the rearview mirror. The noise abruptly ended as the vehicle rolled through the gate at a normal speed and continued until the ambulance stopped close to the plane. A group of people dressed in green scrubs exited the back.

What was going on?

One of the men in the party broke away from the group and started toward her. That must be Tanner. It had been years since she'd seen him. He'd changed as well. His shoulders had broadened and his face had lost its youthfulness, having matured into sharper angles. He was still an extremely handsome man. Maybe even more so now.

With a wide stride that spoke of a person who controlled his realm and was confident to do so, he approached her. She stepped out of the car, closed the door and waited.

"Whitney?"

He didn't recognize her. Was she relieved or disappointed? She extended her hand when he was within arm's reach.

"Whitney Thomason."

Tanner took her hand and pulled her to him, giving her a hug.

What was he doing?

Her face was pressed into the curve of his shoulder. He smelled not of hospital antiseptic but of clean, warm male. Whitney was so surprised her hands fluttered at his waist. What was going on? She was released almost as quickly as he had grabbed her.

Tanner glanced over his shoulder. "Please just go along with me. First names only. No titles."

She looked beyond him to see the others in his party watching them. He made their meeting sound like a covert operation. She took a small step away from him. "Okay. I'm Whitney."

"I'm Tanner. I would prefer we keep my request between the two of us." His dark brown eyes beseeched her.

"I understand. I assure you I am discreet." Most professionals she worked with wanted their interactions with her to remain low-key. Either they didn't want others to know they needed help in their personal life or were just embarrassed they couldn't find someone on their own. Whatever it was, she respected their desires. But no one had gone to the extent that Tanner was to keep his secret.

So why was he meeting her in front of his colleagues? "Then why here?" She nodded her head toward the group at the plane.

"I didn't know I was going to have to go after a heart and I wanted you to get started on this right away."

"After a heart?" Her voice rose.

"I'm a heart transplant surgeon. I'm in the process of retrieving a heart."

"Oh." He made it sound like that was commonplace. For him it might be, but for her it was a little unnerving.

He looked over his shoulder as the jet engines roared to life. "So what do you need from me?"

And he wants to do this right now, right here?

"It usually takes an hour or so for me to get enough information from a client to form a good idea of the type of woman they are best suited to."

Tanner glanced back to where the others were loading the plane. "I don't have an hour. I have a patient who needs a new heart."

"Then I suggest we postpone this meeting." Whitney reached for her car door handle.

"I'd like to get the process started. I'm up for a promotion and the board is breathing down my neck to settle down. I've got to do something right away about finding a wife. But with my caseload I don't know when I'll be able to sit down and talk anytime soon." His voice held a note of desperation that she was confident didn't appear often. "What I'm looking for is someone who takes care of herself, is good in social situations, wants to be a mother and would be supportive of my career."

Really? That's all he wanted? He hadn't said anything about love. This would be a tough order to fill. "Those are pretty broad requirements. I like to know my clients well enough that I don't waste their or their potential partner's time."

"Hey, Tanner," the last man getting on the plane called. "We gotta go. This heart won't wait on us."

Tanner looked back to her. "I've got a patient that's been waiting for months for this heart. I have to see that he gets it. Look, I've heard you're the best in town. Do your thing. I'm sure you can find someone for me. Here's my contact information." He handed her a business card. "Call when you have something. Don't pull away. I'm going to give you a quick kiss on the cheek. I need for these guys—" he nodded toward the plane "—to think that you're my girlfriend."

Before Whitney could agree or disagree, his lips brushed her face and he jogged away.

The man's nerve knew no bounds!

Minutes later Whitney watched as the plane lifted off the ground and flew into the darkening sky. Somehow tonight the Tanner she'd had such a crush on and worshipped in college from afar had become a mortal man. The thing was she really didn't know this Tanner any better than she knew the old Tanner. If she did manage to find him a match, would he take the time to get to know the woman or just expect her to bow to his list of requirements? Whitney's goal was to find love matches, and Tanner had said nothing about wanting that.

And while they worked together there would be no more physical contact. She was a professional.

Tanner looked down from his window seat of the plane at the woman still standing beside her small practical compact car. She looked like a matchmaker. Simply dressed. Nothing sexy or suggestive about her clothing—he'd even characterize her style as unappealing. Her hair was pulled back into a band at her nape.

He didn't go around kissing strangers but he had kissed her. Little Ms. Matchmaker had the softest skin he'd ever felt. She was nothing like the women he was attracted to yet he found her no-nonsense, straight-to-the-point personality interesting. People generally didn't speak to him so frankly.

Did he know her from somewhere? Maybe she'd been a member of one of his former patients' families? But she'd said nothing about knowing him. He was good with faces. It could be her smile that drew him. It was one of the nicest he'd ever seen. Reached her eyes.

He hoped he'd made the right decision in calling her. There had been noises made by the powers-that-be at the hospital that he might be in line for the head of department position when Dr. Kurosawa retired. A subtle suggestion had been made that a settled married man looked more appealing on the vita than a bachelor.

For a moment he'd thought about doing the online dating thing but couldn't bring himself to enter his name. He didn't have the time or inclination to wade through all the possible dates. Make the dates and remake dates. The speed-dating idea came close to making him feel physically sick. Being thought pathetic because he used a dating service also disturbed him. The fewer people who knew what he was doing the better. Truthfully, he was uncomfortable having others know he needed hired help to find a partner. Even employing a matchmaker made him uneasy. But he'd done it. He wanted that directorship.

Finding women to date was no problem for him, but he had never found someone who met his requirements for a lifelong commitment. Tanner wasn't interested in a love match but in a relationship based on mutual life goals. Maybe with the help of an outsider, an impartial one, he could find a woman who wanted the same things he did? The search would be handled like a business, a study of pros and cons.

One thing he did know was that love wouldn't be the deciding factor. He'd already seen what that did to a person. His mother had loved his father but his father had not felt the same. In fact, she'd doted on him, but he'd stayed away more than he'd been at home. Each time he'd left she'd cried and begged him not to go. When he'd leave again she'd be depressed until she learned that he was coming home. Then she'd go into manic mode, buying a new dress and spending hours "fixing herself up." His father had never stayed long. Leaving two boys to watch their mother's misery as he'd disappeared down the drive. Finally he'd divorced her. Tanner refused to have any kind of relationship like that. His career demanded his time and focus. He had to have a wife who could handle that.

Maybe the executive matchmaker could help him find what he needed in a woman. If that woman was happy with what he could offer outside of giving his heart then she would suit him.

"Hey, Tanner," the kidney team surgeon said after a tap to his arm, "who was the woman you were talking to? Did you have to break a hot date?"

He shrugged. "Just a woman I met."

"You know one day you're going to have to settle down. Hospital boards like to have their department heads going home to a family at night. I've got a friend of a friend with a sister. Pretty, I heard."

"I'm good, Charlie."

He grinned. "I'm just saying…"

Tanner was tired of being fixed up by friends and family. Everyone wanted their daughter or friend to marry a doctor.

He looked over at the nurse sitting beside Charlie. She was talking to a member of the liver team. They'd been out a number of times but nothing had really clicked. Tanner didn't want to date out of the nursing pool anymore. He wanted to go home to someone who wasn't caught up in the high adrenaline rush of medical work. A woman who gave him a peaceful haven where he could unwind.

He expected Whitney Thomason to find that person for him.

By the next morning, Tanner had put in over twenty-four hours at the hospital, but his patient, who had been at death's door, was now doing well in CICU. The life-giving gift of a heart transplant never ceased to amaze him. He was humbled by his part in the process.

Thankfully he'd managed to catch a couple of hours' sleep on the plane to and from the hospital where his team had retrieved the heart. Now he had morning rounds to make and then he was headed home to bed. His scheduled surgeries had been moved back a day or postponed. Sleep was the only thing on his agenda for today.

Knocking on the door of Room 223 of the step-down unit, he slowly pushed it open. "Mr. Vincent?"

"Come in." The man's voice was strong.

Tanner entered and moved to the bed. "How're you feeling today, Mr. Vincent?"

"I'd be lying if I said I wasn't sore."

Tanner smiled. Mr. Vincent was only a week out from transplant. Where he'd hardly been able to walk down the hall in the weeks before his surgery, now he could do it back and forth with confidence. Transplants were amazing things. "Sorry about that but it's just part of the process. It should get better every day." Tanner looked around the room. "Mrs. Vincent here?"

"Naw. She had a hair appointment. She doesn't like to miss them." He sounded resigned to his wife's actions. "She'll be here soon, though."

"The plan is for you to go home tomorrow. There are a number of things that the nurses will need to go over with you both."

"Cindy doesn't like blood and all this hospital stuff."

"She'll need to help with your care or you'll have to find another family member to do it. Otherwise home health should be called in."

Mrs. Vincent's self-centeredness was just the type of thing that Tanner couldn't tolerate. This man's wife was so focused on her own needs that she couldn't be bothered to support her husband's return to good health. Her actions reminded him too much of his father's.

"I need to give you a listen, Mr. Vincent." Tanner removed his stethoscope from his neck. After inserting the earpieces in his ears, he placed the listening end on the man's chest. There was a steady, strong beat where one hadn't existed before the transplant.

"Can you sit forward, Mr. Vincent?"

"I can but I won't like it much." The middle-aged man shifted in the bed.

Tanner was listening to the man's lungs when a platinum blonde strolled through the door. She stopped short as if she was surprised to see Tanner.

"Hello, Dr. Locke," she said in a syrupy thick voice.

Tanner had only met Mrs. Vincent a couple of times but each time he had the prickly feeling that she was coming on to him. This time was no different. At least twenty years younger than her husband, she was overdressed and too absorbed in herself for someone who should have been concerned about a husband who had recently been at death's door. Wearing a tight top and pants a size too small, she sauntered up to the bedside, leaning over. Tanner had a view of her cleavage that had no business being shared with anyone but her husband.

More than once Tanner had seen his mother act the same way toward his father. The action then and now made him feel uncomfortable.

"Hi, sweetie. It's nice to see you." Mr. Vincent gave her an adoring smile.

"So how's the patient doing?" she cooed, not looking at her husband. His mother had used that same tone of voice when she'd spoken to his father.

"He's ready to go home after we make sure you both understand his care." Tanner wrapped his stethoscope around his neck.

"I'm not sure I can do that. I'm no nurse. I'm not good with blood and stuff." She gave him a wide, bright, red-painted-lips smile.

Tanner stepped toward the door. "I'm sure the nurses can help you practice so that you become comfortable with what you need to do."

"Cindy, sweetie, we'll figure it out together." Mr. Vincent took her manicured hand and gave her a pleading look. Just the way Tanner's mother had looked at his father before he'd left for weeks.

"I'll let the nurse know that you're ready for her instructions." Tanner went out the door.

The Vincents' marriage was exactly the type he didn't want. The one-sided kind. Tanner was afraid he would be too much like his mother.

Give his heart and have it stomped on. A relationship where one of the partners couldn't see past their love for the other while the other cared about nothing but themselves. A bond based on mutual respect would be far more satisfying in the long run. With his executive matchmaker contacts, that should be just the type of arrangement he'd manage to find.

The censoring look in Whitney's eyes when he'd given his list of requirements had him questioning that she might have expected something more.

Whitney had spent the last two days working through her database in search of women who fit the description of what Tanner wanted. She had five names she thought might be of interest to him. Now she had to pin him down for a meeting so they could start the process.

She picked up the card he'd handed her and tapped it on her desk.

Why couldn't Tanner find his own mate? What was his deal with the passionless list of requirements? He had nothing in common with her in that regard. She was looking for true love. The kind of love that endured forever, no matter what the hardships. The till-death-do-us-part kind that her parents and grandparents had. She'd built her business on that idea. Believed her clients should have that as well.

Once she'd thought she'd had it. That love. With a business degree in hand, she'd taken a job in a corporation. There she'd met Steve. He'd worked in an adjoining department and had seemed not to care that she'd been heavy. That had been a first for her. She'd had no dates in high school and very few in college. When Steve had started giving her attention she'd been ecstatic. For once in her life someone had been interested. After dating for over a year, they'd started planning a wedding.

Two weeks before the ceremony he'd called and told her he'd found someone else. The woman had turned out to be thin and pretty.

Whitney had been devastated. Again that inferiority she'd felt in high school and college had come flooding back. To fight the pain, she'd done whatever she could to keep busy. She'd spent her time walking whenever she'd been alone to prevent dwelling on her broken heart. After a while she'd become interested in wellness nutrition and had adopted a healthy lifestyle. Soon she'd joined an overeating support group and continued to slim down. Men had started paying attention to her but she'd not yet found one that she trusted to stick with her. She wanted a man who cared about her and not just her looks. Those faded.

In college she'd introduced a number of friends to other classmates. The majority of those relationships had become long-term ones and many of the couples had gone on to marry. Whitney had gained the reputation of being a matchmaker. When her boss had confided in her that she was having trouble dating, Whitney had introduced her to a friend of her family. They too had married. A few years later, when the company she'd worked for had downsized and Whitney had been let go, she'd decided that if she couldn't find someone for herself she could at least help others find the right person. Opening Professional Matchmaking had been her answer.

Despite her own disappointments, she still believed that there was a soul mate for everyone. So what had happened in Tanner's life to make him not believe in love? Could she convince him it was necessary for him too? But that wasn't what he was paying her to do. He wanted the best mate possible and it was her job to see that she found that person, not change his requirements.

Whitney punched in Tanner's number from the card. Now it was time to help him do just that.

On the second ring he answered. "Locke."

"This is Whitney Thomason."

"Who?" His voice became muffled, as if he was speaking to someone else.

"Whitney Thomason of Professional Match-making."

"Uh, yeah. Just a minute."

She waited while he spoke to the other person, giving orders about what should be done for a patient.

Even with his abrupt speech he had a nice voice. Sort of warm and creamy. The kind a woman liked to hear in her ear when a man rolled toward her in the middle of the night. Heavens, that wasn't a thought she should be having about her newest client.

Seconds later the background noise quieted.

"I only have a few seconds. What can I do for you?"

She understood about being busy but he was the one requesting her help. "I have compiled a list of possible matches for you. I'd like to get together and discuss them. Start setting up some socials."

"Socials? I'm not interested in, neither do I have time for, tea parties."

That's why he didn't have anyone. He wouldn't put in the effort it took to develop a relationship. "Socials are when you have your first meeting with a potential mate. Before I can set those up we need to talk and sort out who you'd like to consider first."

"Can't you just take care of that?" He already sounded distracted. Maybe he was the same self-centered guy she'd known in college.

"Tanner, are you sure you want to do this?" Her voice took on a hard note. "You have to put some time and effort into finding the right person. Maybe you aren't ready yet."

There was a pause then a sigh of resignation. "What do you want me to do?"

"Can you meet me at Café Lombard at six this evening?"

"I'll be there." There was a click on the line as he ended the call.

Had she made him mad? Her time was valuable too. Tanner had come to her for help. He was going to have to meet her halfway, do his part to help find the perfect match for him. That required energy. If their conversation at the café didn't go well, she'd just tell him that he needed to go elsewhere for assistance.

Café Lombard was a small establishment at the bottom of Lombard Street, which was famous for being the curviest street in the world. Flowers bloomed between each of the curves, making it a fun street to look at but not to drive along. Tanner wasn't a fan of quaintness and this was one of the most picturesque places in San Francisco.

When he arrived right at six, he spotted Whitney sitting at a table for two in the patio area.

Again her shoulder-length hair was primly pulled back into a controlled mass at the nape of her neck. She wore a simple blouse that gave little hint of her body shape and with that were a pair of black pants and flat shoes. There was nothing flamboyant about her. She looked as if she wanted to blend in, go unnoticed.

He started across the street toward her. She glanced up. A smile came to her lips as she waved at him. Now that expression stood out. It encouraged him to return it and he did.

Tanner joined her at the table.

"You're not going to grab me, are you?" She put a chair between them.

"Not unless you want me to. Look, I'm sorry about that. I just didn't want my colleagues asking a lot of questions. It was easier to pretend you were my girlfriend."

"I guess I can understand that."

He dropped into the chair across from her.

"Would you like something to drink or eat? It's on me, of course," Whitney offered.

She seemed to have already forgotten his invasion of her personal space. She was a good sport. "Thank you. I'm starved. But I can get my own."

The waiter came to their table.

"I'll have a cob salad and a water," Whitney said.

"And I'll have a steak sandwich with fries with a large lemonade."

The waiter left. Whitney quirked a corner of her mouth up as if perplexed by something.

"What?" Tanner asked.

"Lemonade? You seem more like a beer guy."

"I am, but I'm on call."

"Ah, that makes sense." She appeared to approve.

He leaned forward and crossed his arms on the table. "I'm sorry I was so abrupt with you on the phone. I've just been super busy this month. Under a lot of pressure."

She smiled. "I understand. I'll try to keep this short and sweet."

"So what did you need to see me about?"

"I've found some potential dates I think you might be interested in. I'd like you to review their files and see what you think. Then I'll set up a social with the one you like best." Whitney pushed a pink folder toward him.

Pink seemed an appropriate color for a matchmaker. At least her office supplies had some flair. Tanner opened the folder to find a printed page with the name of a woman at the top and information about her. He looked at Whitney. "No picture? I don't get to see what they look like?"

"Not until you meet them. I think a lasting relationship should be based on something more than looks. I want my clients to see beyond the surface."

"Interesting." Was there something peculiar about that belief? She no doubt believed in true love and happily-ever-after. He'd learned long ago not to believe in fairy tales. He flipped through the other pages. The women seemed interesting but a couple of them owned their own businesses. He picked up their sheets. "These don't look like they would have time to devote to children, take on social obligations."

"They both assure me that they would be willing to change their lifestyle for the right person. We can put them at the bottom of the list, if you wish, however."

"Have you spoken to them about me?" He didn't relish the idea of being discussed like a piece of merchandise. Yet he was doing the same thing in regards to those women.

She took the women's profiles from him and placed the open file on the table between them both. "I didn't disclose your name or picture but, yes, they have reviewed your profile as well."

"So this is how it works."

"Yes."

The waiter returned with their meals. Neither of them said anything until he left.

Whitney leaned forward with a reassuring smile on her lips. "It's not as painful as you might think. All my clients are interested in finding the same thing. Happiness with someone."

She made it sound like this was about a love match. A ride off into a beautiful sunset. "I'm more interested in someone who's compatible and interested in the same things as I am."

"I think if you spend some time reading this information—" she tapped the folder with her well-manicured, unpolished index finger "—you'll find these are all women worth meeting. They're all very lovely people."

Tanner took a bite out of his sandwich as he flipped the pages back and forth. He continued to eat and review the women's information. A couple of them sounded like they might work. He glanced at Whitney. She was sitting straight with one hand in her lap, eating her salad. Her manners were excellent.

He pushed two sheets toward her. "I think I would like to start with these."

She put her fork down and looked at the papers then nodded. "These are good choices. I'll see about setting up socials. I'll let you know when and where to meet."

"How will I know them?"

There was that reassuring lift of the lips again. "I'll be there to introduce you. It's very uncomfortable to wait for a person you don't know so I'll make the introductions and then leave you to get to know each other."

"So that's all there is to it?" He closed the folder and nudged it back toward her.

She moved her half-eaten salad away and took the folder. "That's it, except for the bill."

He raised a brow and grinned. "I thought you were getting the meal."

"I am, but there's the charge for my services so far." Whitney reached into her purse, removed an envelope and handed it to him.

"Did you add extra for meeting me at the airport and the hug and kiss?"

Whitney pushed the chair back. She looked dead serious when she said, "No. That came for free—once. Next time it will cost you."

"I hope it isn't necessary again. I'll have this in the mail tomorrow." He stuffed the envelope into his pants pocket.

Again she dug into her purse, came out with a couple of green bills and placed them on the table. "Thank you for that. Now, if you'll excuse me, I'll get started on setting up those socials. I'll be in touch soon."

Tanner watched her leave the patio and cross the street. Interesting person. Combination of quiet firmness and solid businesswoman. He grinned. She'd become a little flustered when he'd mentioned that hug and kiss again. There was a softness under that businesswoman tough exterior. His gaze moved to the swing of her shapely hips. That wasn't bad either.

CHAPTER TWO

IT HAD BEEN two days since Whitney had spoken briefly to Tanner about the social she had set up for him today. He'd assured her he would be there but he'd yet to show. She'd always had one of her clients meet her early so that they were waiting for the other one when he or she arrived.

Whitney looked around the coffee shop again. Still no Tanner. Picking up her phone, she texted him.

"Were you worried that I wouldn't show?" a deep voice asked from behind her.

She looked around and into Tanner's dark, twinkling eyes. He had nice eyes. Eyes she suspected saw more than he let on. "I was more worried about your tardiness hurting your chances with Michelle Watkins. After all, we're doing this for you."

"And I appreciate that. It's the reason I am here. So I'm going to be meeting Michelle. Five-six, brown hair, educated at UCLA and likes the outdoors." He came around the table and took the chair across from her.

"I see you remember your facts."

"So what happens now?" He leaned toward her as if what she was going to say was super important. She'd bet he had a great bedside manner.

"When Michelle arrives, I'll introduce you to each other, then I'll leave you to charm her."

His focus didn't waver. "How do you know I can do that?"

Tanner's intense attention made her nerves jump. She'd said more than she'd intended. Would he see the weakness and insecurity she worked to keep at bay? Since he hadn't remembered her she hadn't planned on bringing up their college years. Now she either lied to him or admitted she'd recognized him. She wasn't a liar. With her ex, Steve, she'd lived a lie and wouldn't ever treat anyone that way. "You and I had a few classes together at Berkeley."

He looked truly surprised. Cocking his head to the side, he asked, "We did?"

"Yeah. They were lower-level classes." From there she'd gone into business classes, he into sciences. She'd still seen him around campus, though.

He appeared to give that thought, as if searching back through his memories of those days. "I'm sorry, I don't remember you."

His tone led her to believe he was sincere. "There's no reason that you would."

Tanner leaned back in his chair and studied her. "So how does a woman with an education from Berkeley become a matchmaker?"

"Mostly by accident. I helped some people in college meet someone and then later did the same thing for my boss, and the rest is history."

He nodded sagely. "Just that easily you started a business matching people up?"

"It wasn't all that easy at first. But the word got around that I am discreet and, most of all, successful." She glanced toward the front door then raised her hand, drawing Michelle Watkins's attention.

Tanner looked over his shoulder then quickly stood. Whitney gave him points for being a gentleman. But she wasn't the one he needed to impress. Michelle was. She was smiling, which was encouraging.

When the woman reached them Whitney introduced them. "Michelle, I'd like you to meet Tanner Locke."

Tanner offered Michelle his hand, along with a warm smile that Whitney recognized from their college days when he'd been charming a crowd of women. "It's a pleasure to meet you, Michelle. Please, join us."

Michelle couldn't seem to keep her eyes off

Tanner. Was she already bowled over by him? Whitney was tempted to roll her eyes. The man's magic knew no bounds.

"Thank you," Michelle cooed, and took the chair Tanner held for her.

"Why don't I order us all something to drink?" Whitney suggested as a waitress came to the table.

"That would be nice," Michelle agreed, not taking her gaze off Tanner.

Whitney placed the order and the waitress left.

Tanner looked at Michelle. "I understand you like the outdoors."

"Yes," Michelle simpered. "I love to hike when I have the time."

Whitney sat back and listened as the two traded stories about their favorite hikes. They seemed to have forgotten she was there, something that had happened to her more than once in her life. She'd learned to live with it. This time it was part of her business.

The waitress brought their drinks, which swung Tanner's attention back to her. "Thank you for the lemonade. I'll get these this time," he said to Whitney, then his attention returned to Michelle.

Whitney took a long swallow of the cool, tart liquid. Setting the glass on the table, she said,

"I'll leave you both to get to know each other better. I'll be in touch."

Tanner nodded.

Michelle said, "Thank you, Whitney," before her attention went straight back to Tanner.

Whitney walked to the front door. She looked back at them. They made a nice-looking pair. Two dark-haired, well-groomed, professional people who looked as if they were enjoying each other's company.

That was what her matchmaking was all about. So why couldn't she do that for herself?

Two days later, Whitney answered the phone.

"We need to talk."

Whitney didn't have to question who she was speaking to. She knew that voice at the first roll of a vowel. This time it wasn't warm and creamy. It was icy and sharp.

"Tanner, is something wrong?" She kept her voice low and even. She didn't often have to talk a client down after a social or a date.

"Michelle won't do. We need to meet again. Bring that file."

Whitney stiffened. She wasn't one of his OR nurses to be ordered around. "What's wrong?"

"I don't have time to talk about it now."

And he thinks I do?

"Let me see. How about the coffeehouse on Market Street tomorrow morning around nine?"

"I have surgery then. Could you come to the hospital in about an hour?"

What? She wasn't at his beck and call. She'd already gone out of her way for him once and now he wanted her to drop what she was doing and drive downtown. "I don't know. That isn't how I like to conduct business. I thought you didn't want anyone to know you were using my services. Aren't you afraid someone might ask you questions?"

"They might but I don't have to answer. Whitney, it would really help me out if you could come here. I'm tied up with cases but I'd really like to get this other stuff rolling along."

Other stuff rolling along.

Was that how he thought of the woman who would share the rest of his life? She was glad she didn't fit his list.

Unfortunately, she didn't really have a good excuse why she couldn't help him out. "Okay, but I won't be doing this again."

"Great. Just give me a call when you get here." He hung up.

Tanner hadn't even said goodbye. It was time to have a heart-to-heart with him about whether or not he was really interested in doing the work needed to find a soul mate.

The traffic was light so she made good time going up and down the hills of San Francisco. The city could be difficult to drive in but the views of the bay made it worth it. She was just sorry a streetcar didn't run close enough to the hospital for her to take one of those.

She found a parking spot in the high-rise lot next to the hospital. Crossing the street, she entered the towering hospital. In the lobby, she pulled out her phone and called Tanner's number. Never in her wildest dreams would she ever have imagined having it at her fingertips. She and Tanner didn't move in the same circles and never would.

He answered as he had before. There was an arrogance to how he responded but the crisp sound of his last name seemed to suit him.

"It's Whitney."

"Hey." His tone changed as if he was glad to hear from her. She liked that idea too much. Obviously since he'd gotten his way he had calmed down. "From the main lobby door continue down the long hallway to the second bank of elevators on your right. They'll be about halfway down the hall. Take one of them. Come up to the fifth floor. I'll meet you at the elevator."

Tanner didn't wait for her to answer before closing the connection. That she wasn't as accepting of. She'd rather be told goodbye.

Whitney found the bank of elevators and took the next available car. At the correct floor she stepped off. As good as his word, Tanner stood there, talking to another man also dressed in scrubs. When he saw her he left the man and strolled over to her.

He was the epitome of the tall, dark and handsome doctor. He still had the looks that drew women's attention. What had happened between him and Michelle she couldn't fathom.

Michelle had called yesterday morning all but glowing about the social and the date they'd had the night before. How she could have seen it as being so wonderful while Tanner was so unhappy was a mystery to Whitney.

"Thanks for coming." Tanner ran his hand over his hair. "I know it wasn't what you wanted to do. I had to come in last night to do an emergency surgery. I just couldn't get away today. I have one more patient to see. Would you mind hanging out for a little bit?"

If he'd asked her that in college she might have fainted. Now Whitney only saw him as a man who needed her services. "Sure. I wouldn't mind watching what you do. It might help me better understand you, which would assist me in matching you."

"All business, all the time."

"You're one to be talking," she quipped.

He grinned. "You're not the first person to say that. After I see this patient we'll go to my office to talk."

They walked down a hall until they came to double doors. Tanner scanned a card and the doors opened from the middle out. They entered a hallway with patients' rooms. He stopped at the third doorway along the passage. "This is Mr. Wilcox. Let me get permission for you to come in."

"I don't mind waiting out here."

Tanner touched her arm when she started to move to the other side of the hall. A zing of awareness traveled up her arm. "He's rather lonely. He'd like to have the company. See a face that has nothing to do with the hospital."

That was a side of Tanner she hadn't expected. Compassion beyond the medicine. "Then I'll be glad to say hi."

Tanner raised his hand to knock on the door but turned back to her. "He has a lot of pumps and drips hooked to him. That stuff doesn't bother you, does it?"

She smiled. "No, I promise not to faint or stare."

"Good." Tanner appeared pleased with her answer. Had other women he'd known acted negatively to what he did for a living? He knocked on the door and stuck his head around it. There was a rumble of voices, then Tanner waved her toward him.

"We'll need to wear masks." He pulled a yellow paper one from a box on a table outside the door and handed it to her before entering the room. She followed.

Mr. Wilcox was about her father's age, but his skin was an ash gray. Beside him was a bank of machines with lights. There was a whish of air coming from one. A clear rubber tube circled both the man's ears and came around to fit under his nose.

"Mr. Wilcox, I brought you a visitor," Tanner said.

The man's dull eyes brightened for a second as he looked at her.

"Whitney Thomason, I'd like you to meet Jim Wilcox."

"Nice to meet you, young lady," Mr. Wilcox wheezed as he raised a hand weakly toward her.

"You too, Mr. Wilcox." Whitney stepped closer to the bed.

"So how're you feeling?" Tanner asked, leaning forward, concern written on his face.

Whitney was impressed with the lower timbre of his voice, which sounded as if he truly wished to know. She could grow to admire this Tanner.

"Oh, about the same. This contraption—" Mr. Wilcox nodded toward the swishing machine beside him "—is keeping me alive but I'm still stuck in this bed."

"Well, maybe there'll be a heart soon."

"That's what you've been telling me for weeks now. I'm starting to think you're holding out on me." Mr. Wilcox offered a small smile and perked up when he looked at her. "At least you were kind enough today to bring me something pretty to look at."

Whitney blushed. "Thanks but—"

"Aw, don't start all that stuttering and blustering. I have a feeling your beauty goes more than skin deep."

Whitney really did feel heat in her cheeks then. "I think that might be the nicest compliment I've ever received."

Tanner's eyes met hers and held. Did he agree with Mr. Wilcox? Did he see something that others didn't?

The older man cleared his throat.

Tanner's attention returned to him. "Okay, Romeo. I need to give you a listen." He pulled his stethoscope from around his neck. "I might have done a bad thing by inviting Whitney in."

"If I promise to be nice, will you bring her back again?" Mr. Wilcox asked with enthusiasm in every word.

Whitney touched the older man's arm. "Don't

worry, he doesn't have to invite me for me to come again."

She felt more than saw Tanner glance at her.

"Then I'll look forward to it. So tell me how you know this quack over here?" Mr. Wilcox indicated Tanner.

Her gaze met Tanner's. There was panic in his gaze. He probably didn't want the man to know she was helping him find a wife. "Oh, we were in college together."

Tanner's brows rose. He nodded as if he was pleased with her response.

"Where'd you go?" Mr. Wilcox rasped.

"Berkeley," she told him.

"Then you got a fine education."

Tanner interrupted them with, "So, are you having any chest pains?"

Mr. Wilcox paused. "No."

"That's good. You seem to be holding your own." Tanner flipped through the chart he'd brought in with him and laid it on the bed tray. "You need to be eating more. You have to keep your energy up."

"I'll try but nothing tastes good." Mr. Wilcox pushed at the bed table as if there was something offensive on it.

"Not even ice cream?" Tanner asked.

"I've eaten all those little cups I can stand.

I'd like a good old-fashioned banana split that I could share with someone like your young lady."

Tanner chuckled. "When you get your heart and are out of here I'll see if I can get Whitney to come back and bring you a fat-free split."

"Fat-free," he spat.

"That's it," Tanner said with a grin.

"Well, if Whitney shares it with me maybe I can live with it. She has nice eyes. Windows to the soul, they say." Mr. Wilcox smiled.

"That she does," Tanner agreed.

Whitney looked at Tanner. Did he really mean that? She'd had no indication that he'd noticed anything about her.

"So is she your girlfriend?"

"Just friends," she and Tanner said at the same time.

Whitney wasn't sure that their professional association qualified as friendship. Tanner wanted his personal business kept private, so "friends" seemed the right thing to say. Could they be friends? She didn't know. What she did recognize was that she liked the Tanner who was concerned enough about his patient's loneliness to invite her to meet him just to cut the monotony of being in the hospital day after day. That was a Tanner she could find a match for. Sad that the other Tanner wouldn't let this one show up more often.

"Even behind that mask I can tell she's pretty enough to be your girlfriend. You can always tell a special woman by her eyes. My wife, Milly, had beautiful eyes."

Tanner put his hand on the man's shoulder. "I think we'd better be going."

Whitney touched Mr. Wilcox's arm briefly. "I hope to see you again soon. It was nice to meet you."

He lifted a hand and waved as she reached the door. "You too. You're welcome to my abode anytime."

Whitney smiled. She liked Mr. Wilcox. "Bye, now."

Tanner joined her. "See you soon, Mr. Wilcox."

"You too, Doc."

Whitney stepped out into the hall and Tanner followed, pulling the door closed behind him.

As they removed their masks Tanner said, "I'm sorry if he made you feel uncomfortable in there or put you on the spot about being with me. Mr. Wilcox can be pretty cheeky."

"I didn't mind. He seems like a nice guy who's lonely."

"He is. As a doctor I'm not supposed to have favorites but I really like the man. He's been waiting too long."

She watched for his reaction as she said,

"That's why you took me to see him. You knew he needed something to prick his interest. You didn't mind him assuming I was your girlfriend because that would give him something to figure out, live for."

"Why, Ms. Thomason, you are smart."

Whitney couldn't deny her pleasure at his praise. She also couldn't help but ask, "I know you can't tell me details, but what's going on with Mr. Wilcox?"

Tanner's eyes took on a haunted look. "Most of it you heard. He's waiting for a heart. He needs one pretty quickly."

"Or he'll die," she said quietly.

Tanner's eyes took on a shadowed look. "Yeah."

"You seem to take that in your stride." She sounded as if she was condemning him even to her own ears.

"It's a part of what I do. Medical School 101. But that doesn't mean I like it." His retort was crisp. He started down the hall and she followed. At the desk he handed a nurse Mr. Wilcox's chart and continued on. "My office is this way. I'm on call tonight."

Whitney had to hurry to keep up with him. They walked down a couple of hallways to a nondescript door. Again Tanner swiped his card. There was a click. He turned the doorknob and entered. She trailed him down a short hall to a small sterile-looking office. It became even smaller when Tanner stepped in.

There was a metal desk with a black high-backed chair behind it and a metal chair in front. What struck her as most interesting was the absence of pictures. Didn't he have family? Nieces or nephews? A dog?

"Please, come in." Tanner walked around the desk and settled into the chair. Was his home this cold as well? Could he open his life enough to have a wife and family?

Whitney sat in the uncomfortable utilitarian chair. Apparently whoever visited wasn't encouraged to stay long. "I understand from Michelle that she had a wonderful time the other night. So what's the problem on your side?"

Tanner picked up a pen and twisted it through his fingers, a sure sign he wasn't comfortable with the question. "She wanted something that I won't give."

There was a chilly breeze in the words. "That is?"

"Let's just say she was already getting more emotionally attached than I want to be. You need to go through your file and find me some women who are interested in security, financial comfort, social status, not whether or not they are loved.

I'm looking for something far more solid than love. Companionship."

Whitney felt like she'd been punched in the chest. She'd never heard anything sadder. All the compassion she'd just seen Tanner show Mr. Wilcox was gone. Now all she saw was a shell of a man. For him a heart was nothing more than an organ that pumped blood. Not the center of life she believed it to be. "The women I represent all want to be loved."

He put his elbows on the desk and steepled his fingers, giving her a direct look. "For the amount of money I'm paying you I expect you to find someone who suits my needs. I thought I'd made it clear what I wanted in a relationship. It's your business to find me that match."

If he had slapped her she couldn't have been more insulted. "I assure you I know my business. I'll set up a social with the next client on my list for as soon as possible." She looked him in the eyes. "But you should know, Tanner, it's my experience that most people see marriage less as a business deal and more as an emotional attachment."

Tanner's face turned stern. His voice was firm when he said, "That might be the case but that isn't the type of person I'm looking for. I've made my request and you've stated you can fill it, so that's what I expect."

What had happened to the man? How could he be so compassionate toward his patient but so calculating about the type of wife he wanted? Whitney stood. "I'll be in touch soon."

He got to his feet as well. "Good. If you take a right out of my door you'll come to a set of elevators. It'll take you down to the lobby. Thanks for coming here."

She'd been dismissed. That was fine with her. Whitney turned on her heel and left. Right now she wasn't sure if she should keep Tanner as a client. Truth be known, she wasn't certain she even liked him.

Tanner was at Café Lombard for the "social" before Whitney or the woman he was to meet. When Whitney had left his office the other evening she hadn't been happy. Her lips had been pinched tight and her chin had jutted out. Somehow what he had said she had taken personally. Hadn't he made it clear what he was looking for in a relationship during their earlier interview? Couldn't she understand that he had no interest in a love match?

Those only led to pain, not just between the husband and wife but for the children as well. He and his brother were a prime example of that. They hadn't seen each other in years. Tanner wanted a marriage based on something solid and not fleeting, like an emotion.

His date with Michelle had been wonderful. They'd had a number of things in common. They both enjoyed the outdoors, liked baseball and traveling. It wasn't that he didn't like Michelle, but he could tell by her speech and her body language that she was looking for more than he could give. There had been hopeful stars in her eyes. He wanted someone whose expectations were less dreamlike and more firmly rooted in reality.

Statements like "Children should know that their parents care about each other. It makes for a more stable child," or "I want a husband who can be there when I need him," showed him that Michelle needed emotional support that he just couldn't give. Tanner wanted someone who could handle their own ups and downs without involving him.

He looked up to see Whitney entering. The displeased expression she'd worn the other day was gone but there was still a tightness around her lips, indicating she might not be in the best of moods. When had he started being able to read so well someone he hardly knew?

He half stood. She flashed a smile of greeting. It was an all-business tilt of the lips instead of actual gladness to see him. Tanner didn't much care for that. Yet why did it bother him to have her disgruntled with him?

Today Whitney wore a flowing dress with a small pale pink rose pattern on it that reached just past her knees. A sweater was pulled over her shoulders and the sleeves tied across her chest. She was dressed like an old-maid schoolteacher. Why did she wear such nondescript clothing? Did she do it because she thought people believed that was how a matchmaker should dress? She was too young and too attractive not to flaunt it some. What would she look like in a tight, short skirt? He'd be interested to see. Great, would be his guess. But why should it matter to him how she dressed?

"Hello, Tanner." She took the chair across from him. "You're early."

"My last case was canceled due to a fever so I got away from the hospital sooner than I thought I would."

Whitney clasped her hands in her lap and looked directly at him. "I think you work too hard and too many hours." It wasn't an accusation, more a statement of fact. She didn't give him time to respond before she continued. "You're going to meet Racheal today. I think you'll really like her. She has a master's degree in business and loves children."

"I remember reading her profile. Did you make it clear to her what I am looking for?"

"I did. She's interested in a family but doesn't want to give over her freedom just to have that. She's looking for the same type of relationship that you are." Whitney made it sound as if the idea left a bad taste in her mouth.

"Do you have a problem with that?"

She shrugged then leaned back in the chair. "Not if that's what you both want."

He leaned forward, piercing her with a look.

She shifted in the chair.

Tanner crossed his arms on the table. "Tell me what you think this should be about."

Her eyes widened. She did have pretty ones. Like green grass after spring rain. She blinked. "It isn't about what I think but about what you want."

"Spoken like a true matchmaker, eager to please. Are you married, Whitney?"

Her chin raised a notch. "I don't believe that has anything to do with your case."

"It might not but it gives me an idea of how good you are at this matchmaking business."

She shifted in her chair. "If you don't have any confidence if my ability then I'll be glad to refund your money minus five hundred dollars for the work I've done so far."

He'd hit a touchy spot. "And add the charge for the hug and kiss after all?"

She relaxed and shook her head. "No. I wouldn't do that. This isn't a joke."

He leaned back in the chair and watched her for a long moment. Her direct look challenged his. This was a woman who wouldn't give up until she had succeeded. "You're right—it isn't. I'm not ready to throw in the towel yet."

"Then you do understand that I have the same responsibility to the women I introduce you to as I do to you?"

She had backbone and a moral line. What you saw was what you got with Whitney. That was refreshing. Most women he knew were only really interested in themselves. "I realize that. I'll try to be on my best behavior."

"I'm starting to wonder what that is. I also expect you to give them a fair chance." Her tone had become schoolmarmish.

"You don't think I gave Michelle that?"

She didn't immediately answer. "Truthfully, I'm not sure you did."

It didn't matter to him if she thought so or not. He knew what he wanted better than she did, matchmaker or not. It was his life they were talking about. He'd seen what uninvited and unrequited love did to a person. He wanted none of it. Good, solid, practical thought was what his marriage would be based on.

A blonde woman stepped up to their table. Whitney jerked around as if she'd forgotten all about her joining them. Tanner smiled. She'd been too flustered by his questions to remember why they were there. He liked the idea that he'd rattled Whitney. Too much.

"Hello, Racheal. I'm sorry I didn't see you when you came in." Whitney's voice sounded a little higher than normal.

Once again, Whitney was a contrast to her female client. Racheal had a short haircut and every strand was in its place. Her makeup was flawless and she wore the latest fashion with ease. She certainly looked the part of the woman he thought he would like to share his name. He looked at Whitney and somehow he found her more to his taste. Shaking that thought away, Tanner returned his attention to Racheal.

He stood and offered his hand to her. "Tanner Locke. Thanks for joining us."

He held a chair out for Racheal and she gracefully slipped into it.

"It's nice to meet you." Racheal had a no-nonsense note in her voice.

He looked at Whitney. "I've already ordered drinks."

"Thank you, Tanner. I think I'll leave you and

Racheal to get to know each other better. I'll be in touch soon."

Tanner remained standing as she left. A tug of disappointment went through him to see her go. Why?

Whitney hadn't heard from Tanner in three days. Far too often she had found herself wondering how things were going between him and Racheal. She liked to give her clients time to get to know each other and digest their thoughts on the new match before she asked. This time she was particularly anxious to know.

Racheal had already checked in. She seemed pleased with Tanner. According to her, they'd had a wonderful time talking at the social and had enjoyed their first date. Maybe she had found the right one for Tanner after all. But she had thought that with Michelle. She would wait until tomorrow and give him a call. See if he was as pleased as Racheal.

That evening Whitney was just slipping into bed when her phone rang. A call this late usually didn't mean good news. Was her father ill again? "Hello?"

"It's Tanner."

His voice was low and gravelly. There was no apology for calling so late. She wasn't surprised.

But with his schedule he probably thought nothing of it. "Yes?"

"You told me to call and let you know how things are going."

She had indeed told him that but had assumed he would do so during business hours. An edgy feeling washed over her, knowing she was in bed while talking to Tanner. It seemed far too evocative. She flipped the covers back and stood beside the bed.

"Racheal seems to be working out. We went out last night. I have a party on Friday that I've invited her to." His voice was low and calm, as if he had all the time in the world to talk.

"I'm glad to hear it. I'll check in with you both next week. I look forward to hearing how the relationship is progressing."

"How have you been?" His voice was warm and silky.

Whitney walked to the window. "I'm fine."

"That's good. Goodnight."

Whitney listened to the click on the other end of the line. She returned to her bed and pulled the covers over herself again. Somehow the sheets didn't feel as cool anymore.

Maybe Racheal was it. Had Tanner found the one he wanted? Whitney wished she felt happier about that idea.

Even if he hadn't, he wouldn't look at her that

way. Did she want him to? Turning off the light, she settled under the covers, but it took her far too long to fall asleep.

Whitney continued to wonder how things were going between Tanner and Racheal. More than once she'd been tempted to call him but had held back. She'd never had that problem before. Normally she let her couples go without thought or overseeing them, but Tanner's case held too much of her attention.

Whitney was already asleep a week later when the phone rang. She picked up the phone and a man's voice said, "Just what type of women are you introducing me to? You're supposed to be the best at this."

"Tanner, what's going on? Do you know what time it is?"

"Yes. I know what time it is." He sounded angry.

At this point the time didn't matter. She was awake anyway. Despite that, she found herself happy to finally hear from him. "What's the problem?"

"The problem is that Racheal backed out of a weekend we had planned in Napa. It's a hospital retreat and I had already said I would be bringing a guest. I'm trying to make a positive impression on the board. This situation could hurt my chance for a promotion."

"I'm sorry." And she was. He was a good doctor and deserved it, she was sure.

"You should be. I hold you responsible."

"Me!" Whitney squeaked and set up in bed.

"I'm paying you to provide me with women who understand the importance of my job and position."

What was he raving about? "Racheal didn't?"

"I guess not. She agreed to go and now at the last minute she's backed out."

Whitney worked to keep her tone even. "Did she give you a reason?"

"She just said she wasn't ready for this step."

That sounded reasonable to Whitney. "You can't expect her to do something that she isn't comfortable with."

"I damn well can expect her to keep her word."

He had a point there, but what did he imagine she could do about it? She couldn't make Racheal go with him. "I have to honor what my clients feel they need to do."

"And you have to honor our contract. I need someone as my girlfriend this weekend."

It was Thursday. How was she going to find someone who would go away with a perfect stranger on such short notice? "I wish I could help you, Tanner. At this point I don't know what I can do."

"Well, I do. If you can't find me someone then you have to come. At least that way I'll be bringing a guest. I can make up a story about how we broke up later."

What? Is he crazy? Spend a weekend with him?

"That's not possible. It's unethical. You're my client."

"One you're expected to keep happy. You were supposed to vet the women you introduce me to. You failed in determining Racheal's true character. I expect you to meet your professional obligation."

How did that logically extend to her personally replacing a client?

"Look, this weekend is important to my career, just as finding the right woman is. There will be no expectations on my part except for you to be pleasant and act as if we're a couple." His voice was firm and determined, as if he wouldn't accept no as an answer.

Whitney's heart pounded. Was she seriously going to consider it? "You can't just demand that I spend the weekend with you."

"Sure I can." His voice had turned hard. "We have a contract for services and you need to hold up your end. It was your suggestion that I pick

Racheal. She didn't hold up her end so that defaults to you."

Whitney wasn't sure she agreed with his reasoning but she didn't need him bad-mouthing her around town. She'd taken Tanner on as a client to increase her professional profile, not to hurt it. Plus, she hated that he was in a spot.

If she agreed to his demand she couldn't imagine the weekend being anything but long and miserable. She didn't belong in his social group. She was an outsider. Tanner wanted someone who could make a good impression. More than once she'd been judged by her looks. He needed someone who could influence. That wasn't her. She was good with people one on one but not as a member of a house party. To run in Tanner's world...

"I'll pick you up at nine in the morning. What's your address?"

"Tanner, I can't do this."

"Oh, yes, you can," he all but hollered down the phone.

He wasn't going to allow her a way out. Apprehension bubbled in Whitney as she gave him her address.

"You'll need a cocktail dress, swimsuit and casual clothes." There was a click on the other end of the line. Tanner had hung up. Once again.

Whitney lay there. What had just happened?

She'd just gotten press-ganged into a weekend with Tanner as his "plus one." What was he thinking? What *was* she doing?

Those bubbles combined into a heavy mass of dread in her chest. She wasn't part of Tanner's world. What if she made a mistake and embarrassed him?

If she had really changed from that insecure girl from years ago it was time to prove it.

CHAPTER THREE

TANNER DIDN'T KNOW what had gotten into him when he'd insisted that Whitney join him on this weekend retreat. He had been so angry when Racheal had called and told him that she wouldn't be going that he'd picked up the phone and dialed Whitney's number without a thought. But to insist she attend a weekend with him might have been overreacting. Desperation had fueled his demand. He needed a woman on his arm.

Well, it was done now.

For him to have a "significant other" with him for the weekend was an unwritten requirement. Besides, he might have hinted to one or two of the board members that he'd become serious about someone. It mustn't look like he'd been lying or he could kiss that promotion goodbye.

He pulled his car to the curb in front of Whitney's home. To his surprise, he'd known the address. She lived in one of the famous "painted ladies." Whitney stood waiting in front of a light blue Victorian row house with a yellow door and white gingerbread trimmings. Pink flowers grew in pots on the steps. The house was an obvious reflection of Whitney. He'd always liked these old homes. Something about them said life was peaceful inside.

Whitney looked small compared to the towering three-story home. His heart fell. This wasn't good. She wore a full shirt that hung almost to her knees and underneath she wore baggy pajama-style pants and flat slippers. Her hair was pulled back into a bun. Whitney couldn't have looked more nondescript if she had tried. He really couldn't force her to dress better, or could he?

Stepping out of the car, Tanner went to the trunk and opened it.

Whitney joined him with her bags in her hand. "Tanner, I think we should really reconsider this idea."

"I've already done that a couple of times and I don't see another way. I need a girlfriend for this weekend and you are it." Even if her sense of style was missing.

Uncertainty filled her eyes. "This type of thing really isn't me."

"You'll be fine. Sitting by the pool and reading all day works for me. I just need you to attend the dinner this evening and tomorrow evening and all will be good."

She didn't look any more enthused but she let him take her bags and climbed into the car.

Yet again he felt bad about insisting she come with him, but he needed her. The board members would be at this retreat and he had to give them the impression he was getting close to settling down. "Do you mind if I put the top down? It's a beautiful day."

"Not at all. I love a convertible."

Tanner leaned over her to unlock the roof from the windshield. A floral scent that fit her perfectly assaulted his nose. Maybe the weekend wouldn't be so bad. He flipped the other lock above his head. When he pushed a button, the roof slowly folded down behind them.

"I like your car. It suits you," Whitney said.

"Thanks. I grew up wanting one of these and when I finished medical school I bought one."

"I've always loved two-seaters. I'm going to enjoy riding in this one." She gave him a weak smile.

So at least they had that in common. As Tanner started the car, Whitney pulled a long multicolored scarf out of her purse. With deft efficiency she wrapped it around her head and tied it under her chin. Great, now he had Old Mother Hubbard with him. Why did she dress like she did?

"The only complaint I have about having the top down is that it's hard on a hairdo."

He'd never really thought of her as having a hairstyle. Her hair had always been just pulled back behind her neck when he'd seen her. Today was no different. She didn't seem to make any real effort to stand out where her appearance was concerned. What was she hiding from? Now with the scarf around her head she looked drabber than ever. That was with the exception of when she smiled. At those times she captured his attention completely.

It disturbed him on a level he didn't want to examine how much time he'd spent thinking about his matchmaker in the past few weeks. Even when he and Racheal had been dating he'd wondered what Whitney would think about this or that, or what she was doing. These were not things his mind should have been contemplating. Racheal had seemed perfect for him, just what he'd asked for, so why had he been thinking about another woman?

Especially Whitney. There could never be any real interest there. They clearly didn't want the same things out of a relationship. He had no plans to ever love a woman. His parents had seen to that.

Tanner's attention remained on his driving as he made his way up and down the steep streets of

San Francisco lined with houses and businesses. He glanced at Whitney a couple of times. She seemed absorbed in the city life around them. Once he caught her looking at him. She made him feel both uncomfortable and pleased.

As they waited at the toll booth at the Golden Gate Bridge she said, "I love this bridge. It's like this big smiling sentinel standing over the bay, protecting it."

"I've never thought about it like that. For me it's a feat of engineering, from the rock foundation to the suspension towers to the length of the wires."

"Or maybe it's like a big swing. Either way, it's amazing."

Tanner looked at her and grinned. "Agreed."

"Did you know that as soon as they finish painting it they have to start over again?" Whitney had her neck craned back, looking up at one of the three soaring towers.

He smiled. "I did. That's a lot of red paint."

Tanner paid the toll and they started across the bridge.

Halfway over the bay Whitney said, "The thump-thump of the tires reminds me of a heartbeat." A few seconds later she continued, "It's mind-boggling to me that I actually know someone who has held a heart in his hand."

Tanner grinned. "I'm glad I can impress." He

wasn't sure he had so far during their acquaintance.

Traffic was heavy, even for a Friday morning, as people were leaving the city for the weekend. The road widened and the driving became easier after they were over the bridge. Tanner had been accused of being a fast driver but Whitney didn't seem bothered by his weaving in and out of traffic. Her hands remained in her lap and her chin up as if she were a flower enjoying the sunshine.

As they headed off the bridge toward the green rolling hills on the way to Napa she asked, "So what's expected of me this weekend?"

"Mostly to act as if you like me."

She met his eyes. "I'll try."

For some reason it disturbed him that she didn't already like him. "I know I've been a little high-handed a couple of times—"

Her brows rose. "A couple? How about all the time?"

Tanner shrugged a shoulder as he changed lanes. "Okay, maybe I deserve that, but I really need your help this weekend."

"You could have asked."

He glanced at her. "Would you have done it?"

"No…" The word trailed off.

Tanner's focus went back to the black sedan he was following. "So I would've had to apply pressure anyway. How about I double your fee for your trouble?"

She shook her head. "Let me think about it. No. That would make me feel like a prostitute."

He didn't like her accusation at all. "Whoa, that isn't what this is about. You won't be expected to sleep with me. In fact, I don't expect you to do anything more than hold on to my arm and pretend to be my girlfriend." Turning left, he followed a sign to Napa.

"Sleeping with you wasn't what I was referring to. I have no intention of doing that."

She made it sound as if he wasn't good enough for her. That was a first for him. Women were usually more than eager to climb into his bed. Why wouldn't she be? Was she holding on to her favors until she found that "love" she was so fond of believing in? Maybe he was just the person to change her mind.

Wait, that wasn't what this weekend was about. He'd promised sex wouldn't be on the agenda. He had no business thinking that way. Whitney was his matchmaker, and only with him because he had insisted. This wasn't some weekend fling. He had to remember that.

"So what're the sleeping arrangements?" Whitney asked in the matter-of-fact way he'd come to expect from her.

"We'll have to share a room but I'll give you as

much privacy as possible. I'll sleep on the floor if necessary." That he wasn't looking forward to. But she was doing him a favor so it was the least he could do to try to make her as comfortable in the situation as possible.

"And what're the other plans for the weekend?"

"There is a round of golf organized for this afternoon and tomorrow." The land flattened as they entered the valley, allowing him to look at Whitney more often.

She met his look. "Do you play golf?"

"Not really. But I'll make a showing just to be a team player." Why did he feel like she was accusing him of being dishonest?

"I wouldn't have thought that was your style. Impressing the board really is important to you, isn't it?"

"It is." Tanner straightened in the seat a little. He wasn't ashamed of it. The promotion meant everything to his career.

"Is the department head position so vital?"

He felt her studying him. "Yes. It's my chance to make a difference in my field. Help people. I can influence the way we do transplants, lead the development of new skills."

"That's to be admired." He heard the approval in her voice.

Tanner glanced at her. He rather liked the glow of respect in her eyes.

Whitney couldn't keep the sigh of pleasure from rushing out of her as they drove up a long lane lined with neat row after row of vines for as far as she could see. The contrast of the deep brown of the rich dirt, the vivid green of the grape leaves and the tranquil blue of the sky was almost breathtaking. She glanced at Tanner.

And she was spending a weekend here with him. Her life had become surreal. She was off with a man that she hardly knew, pretending to be his serious girlfriend, and in a social situation she wasn't comfortable in. How was she not going to make a mess of it?

"Ever been to Napa?" Tanner asked, without taking his eyes off the road.

"Not really."

"I think you'll like it. We're staying at a vineyard with a hotel attached. One of the board members owns it. I understand there's a pool, tennis courts, a spa and just about anything else you might like. And, of course, there's wine."

He made it sound like she would be on her own most of the time, which suited her just fine. She didn't consider herself much of an actress so trying to convince people of the improbable idea that she and Tanner were a couple was distressing.

Finally they drove out of the vines into an open space where a huge structure that looked like a French château stood. Tall, thin trees flanked it on both sides and a manicured yard begged for Whitney to lie in the emerald-colored grass. If she'd been impressed with the landscape on the drive here, this view made her catch her breath. It was picture-perfect and despite the reason she was there Whitney could hardly wait to see inside.

Tanner leaned over and said close to her ear. "See, it's not going to be all bad, being here with me."

Whitney turned. Her mouth stopped only inches from his. Her heart fluttered. She looked into his velvety brown eyes. They could swallow her up if she let them and she would never know how it had happened. For long moments, though far too short for her, she waited, watched. Dreamed. Tanner's head lowered a fraction. He was going to kiss her. No, this wasn't what this weekend was about.

She blinked and quickly pulled back. She wouldn't be his plaything. She wasn't in his league when it came to casual affairs, she was sure. He would win every time. "I didn't say it was going to be bad. I just don't like being told what I'm going to do."

He leaned back and looked at her. "Noted. With that in mind, I'm asking you, not telling, would you please take off that hideous scarf before someone comes out?"

Whitney didn't have time to reply before the door to the hotel opened and a sophisticatedly dressed woman started their way. Quickly Whitney removed the scarf and the band securing her hair. Shaking it loose, she ran a hand through it. She looked to Tanner. "Better?"

A strange look had come over his face and he said softly, "Much." Seconds later a crease marred his forehead. "Can we keep what you do for a living between ourselves?"

"I won't lie."

His look held hers. "Maybe just evade the question."

A young man in a knit shirt and khaki pants followed close behind the woman. This was a far fancier place than Whitney had expected.

"Hello, Tanner. Welcome to the Garonne Winery," the woman said warmly as Tanner stepped out of the car.

The young man opened Whitney's door for her. She said, "Thank you," and received a warm smile.

"Marie Jarvis, I'd like you to meet Whitney

Thomason," Tanner said from the other side of the car.

Marie stepped to Whitney with a well-manicured hand extended. "It's so nice to meet a special friend of Tanner's."

Whitney smiled and took her hand. Marie had no idea just how *special* a friend Whitney was.

Marie waved Tanner away from the trunk of the car. "Kevin will see to your bags and park your car. Just come join us by the pool. We have cool drinks waiting."

"That sounds lovely," Whitney said.

Tanner offered her an encouraging smile. On their way to the door he took her hand. His touch sent a tingle of awareness through her. It was so powerful that for a second she almost jerked away. Remembering they had to pretend they were a couple, she got control of herself. She hadn't counted on her body's reaction to being in such close contact with Tanner. Or how hard she would have to work to remember his touches were just for show. She tried to appear relaxed but her insides were a jumble of knotted nerves. Tanner gave her fingers a squeeze. Did he sense the effect he was having on her?

He allowed her to enter ahead of him through the tall double doors that opened into the cool dimness of the château. The entrance hall was every bit as astounding as the outside. A wrought-iron staircase circled up on both sides of the foyer to a landing. On each side of the landing were large windows with heavy drapes. From there, the stairs climbed again to branch off right and left. To one side of the foyer there was a small Queen Anne–style desk with an attractive young woman seated behind it.

Marie waved in the woman's direction and she smiled before Marie said to them, "Don't worry about checking in. I've already taken care of everything."

Kevin moved across the gray tile floor past them, laden with baggage, and headed up the stairs.

"The pool is this way." Marie walked toward the back of the building.

As they stepped out into the bright light once more, the scene reminded Whitney of a 1940s picture of a movie star's pool. The men stood in groups, talking, with drinks in their hands while the women sunbathed on loungers.

A flutter of anxiety went through her. She was in over her head. Could she get out of this now? What did she have in common with these people? Tanner expected her to mix and mingle. How was she supposed to do that?

When she would have pulled her hand out of Tanner's he gripped it tighter. Had he read her mind and been afraid she might run? Somehow his clasp gave her confidence. Taking a deep breath, Whitney reminded herself that she was no longer that overweight girl who'd felt inadequate for so long. Or at least she didn't plan to let anyone make her feel that way. She was educated, owned her own business and paid her bills. There was nothing for her to feel ashamed of.

Marie said, "Tanner, why don't you introduce Whitney around then you both can change into your bathing suits and join us."

Whitney scanned the area. Even the women who were twice her age seemed to have better bodies than she did. Stretch marks and extra skin still plagued her, despite the number of years that had passed since she'd lost so much weight. Wearing a swimsuit in front of these people, particularly Tanner, wasn't something she was interested in doing.

Tanner's hand on her waist directed her toward the closest group of people. She wasn't used to his touch and certainly not to her reaction to it. If the situation didn't make her nervous enough, Tanner's close proximity did. Why? She wasn't even sure she liked him.

As they approached the group the circle opened to include them.

A man with more white than dark hair and a round belly stepped forward. "Tanner, glad you could make it."

"Malcolm, thanks for having us." Tanner gave her a slight nudge. "I'd like you to meet Whitney. Whitney, this is Malcolm Jarvis, the chairman of the hospital board and the owner of the Garonne Winery. Best known, though, as Marie's husband."

"Yes, yes. Good to meet you." Malcolm smiled at her.

Whitney couldn't help but return one of her own. "Nice to meet you as well. You have a beautiful place here."

"Thank you. Please, make yourself at home this weekend. All the hotel amenities are open to you while you're here."

Tanner faced another man. "This is Dr. Russell Karr, the medical chair and my boss."

Dr. Karr offered his hand. She took it and received a firm shake as he said, "Nice to meet you, Whitney. I look forward to getting to know you."

"And I you." To her amazement she'd managed to say that without her voice wavering.

His hand still on the small of her back, which was surprisingly reassuring, Tanner guided her around the pool. He introduced her to each guest, which included Sue Ann, Russell's wife, Ellen and Carlos Gonzales, and Lucy and Rick Hunt.

A woman close to their age, wearing a skimpy

yellow bikini, stood as Whitney and Tanner came around the end of the pool toward her lounger. She rushed to Tanner and threw her arms around his neck.

Something about their friendliness said there was history between them. Whitney's radar went off. She wasn't going to like this person. Why should it matter what their relationship had been? Tanner didn't belong to her.

"Hello, Charlotte." Tanner's voice didn't sound as warm as her hug would suggest. He removed her arms and stepped away. "I'd like you to meet my girlfriend, Whitney Thomason."

The word *girlfriend* had rolled off his tongue as if it were the truth. Had he put extra emphasis on the word as well? It took all of Whitney's willpower not to stare at him as he continued, "Whitney, this is Charlotte Rivers. Her fiancé is Max Little and *he* is a member of the board. By the way, where is Max?"

Charlotte looked at Whitney as if she were something she would pull off the bottom of her shoe. "He'll be here later this evening. There was a last-minute case."

Not a good history, would be Whitney's guess.

"I know about those. We're going in to get settled. Maybe be out for a swim later." Again, Tanner's hand came to Whitney's waist. For some

reason it gave her a sense of satisfaction to know Tanner was leaving with her. She held her head just a little bit higher.

When they were out of hearing distance from anyone Whitney said, "I don't think Charlotte likes me too much."

"I wouldn't worry about it."

"She's not going to sneak into our room in the middle of the night and take a knife to me and hop into bed with you, is she?"

Tanner stopped walking, threw his head back and let out a huge belly laugh. Hardly able to contain his mirth, he said, "Why, Ms. Matchmaker, I had no idea you had such a sense of the dramatic. I promise to be the one to open the door if anyone knocks. Feel safer now?"

She grinned. "A little." After a moment she dared to ask, "So what's the story with her?"

"Let's just say she doesn't like being turned down when she wants something." Putting his arm around her shoulder, he pulled her to him. This was a friendly action of two people conspiring together.

Maybe they could be friends.

Warmth entered Tanner's voice when he said, "I don't know if I said it but thanks for coming with me this weekend."

"I didn't know that I had a choice."

He held the door as they stepped inside. "I'm afraid you're right about that. But I do hope it isn't too awful for you."

Tanner was pleased with Whitney's reception by his colleagues. They had seemed to like her and she'd handled herself well, even with Charlotte. She had easily read the tension between Charlotte and him and had managed to make a joke out of it. That was a talent he admired. At his guffaw of laughter everyone had looked. To them they must have appeared as two lovers enjoying themselves.

In the house again they passed Kevin going to the front door and he told them what room they were in. Tanner led Whitney up the stairs, to the right and down the hallway to a door at the end. He opened it wide in order to allow her to enter first. When she hesitated he looked back to find her staring at the opening.

"I'm not so sure about this," she said, shaking her head slightly.

"The weekend, the room or staying with me?"

"How about all of it?"

Tanner glanced down the hall. Thank goodness no one was around. "At least come in to talk about it."

He reached for her but she stepped away. His hand fell to his side. After a moment she entered.

He joined her and closed the door. Unsure what to do to make her feel more comfortable, he simply waited near the door.

Whitney's attention appeared fixated on the queen-size four-poster bed against the far wall. Thankfully there was a small sofa under one of the windows. That would be his sleeping spot for the next three nights. Not that he was looking forward to it.

"Why don't we have a seat?" He pointed toward the sofa.

She moved as if her shoes were weights. There she sat on the edge of the cushion, looking as if she would run at any moment. Finally she said, "I'm not particularly comfortable with lying to all these people."

A little charm and persuasion was needed here. "Have we lied? I introduced you as a girlfriend. I don't think that's such a stretch."

"We're really more like colleagues, though."

Whitney wouldn't be an easy sale. "Okay, colleagues. Still we can be friends."

"Those usually know more about each other than we do. I know little about you and you know nothing about me."

"Sure I do. You're a businesswoman with the ability to read people. You understand what helps people relax. You know how to put them at ease. And you like nice cars. You did great back there, by the way." Why was she all of a sudden so antsy? She'd seemed confident at the pool. Was she afraid to be alone with him? Did she sense his physical reaction to her?

When he'd initially placed his hand on her waist it had been for show, but as they'd made their way around the pool, and especially in front of Charlotte, it had become a protective action. Whitney pulled at something in him that he had no intention of examining or exploring.

She scooted back on the sofa, resting more easily in the cushions. "If you don't mind, I would rather not go to the pool. I'll just stay here and unpack."

He wouldn't push her. For now he'd just let her get used to the idea of being here with him. "That's fine. I'll see what Marie has planned for this evening and come back to get you."

"Okay."

"Is there anything special you would like to do while we're in Napa? We don't have to be underfoot here all the time." Maybe if they did something she enjoyed she would settle down some. He certainly didn't need her panicking and heading back to San Francisco.

"I don't know." She pursed her lips. "Maybe a tour of the winery?"

"Sounds good to me. If one isn't planned then we'll take one ourselves."

She smiled but it didn't reach her eyes.

"I'll leave you to unpack." He headed for the door. "I'll see you in a little while."

Tanner returned an hour later to find Whitney asleep in the middle of the bed. It was early for a nap. Had she been up the night before, worrying about coming with him this weekend? Through their meetings she'd proved herself intelligent and a woman who took little guff from people, or at least him. So why wouldn't she take the weekend at face value? Was she that distrustful of men or just him? She didn't strike him as insecure.

Why did he care? He had no intention of becoming emotionally involved with Whitney. The more he knew about her the more invested he would be in her life. He didn't want or need that. In fact, that implied caring and he wasn't going to take that step. Caring equated to hurt. He'd seen that clearly with his parents.

They'd get through this weekend and go back to being matchmaker and client.

Whitney looked so peaceful that he hated to wake her but Marie had made plans for everyone that afternoon. He placed a hand on Whitney's shoulder and gave her a gentle shake. She blinked then her eyes popped wide open. They were pretty eyes, almost as nice as her smile. The kind that saw into a person.

"Hey, the women are going into town for lunch

and some shopping while the men go to the club to play golf."

"Is it necessary for me to go?" she asked after a yawn.

"If you don't mind, I wish you would. I wouldn't want to hurt Marie's feelings." Tanner wouldn't make it a demand. He'd made enough of those.

"Oh, of course." Sitting up and trying to unrumple her clothing, she said in a convincingly sincere tone, "I don't want to do that either."

If anything, Whitney had a kind heart. Maybe that was why her business as a matchmaker was so successful.

"I'll tell you what—" he reached for his wallet in his back pocket "—why don't you buy something nice for yourself? It's the least I can do for you helping me out this weekend."

"That's not necessary."

"Maybe not, but I'd like to. You could maybe get a new outfit." He shrugged a shoulder. "Something more fitted."

Whitney raised a brow. "Thank you but I don't need you to buy clothes for me."

"I just thought you might enjoy going more if you could buy something new."

She rolled off the bed and faced him. "I don't need your money."

Tanner held up a hand. "Whoa, whoa. I didn't

intend to insult you. Whatever you wear is fine with me. I was just thinking you must be covering up some nice curves under those loose-fitting clothes." He handed her a few bills. "Just take this. Get whatever you want. Or don't. Marie said to meet in the lobby in half an hour. I'll see you later."

He was out the door before she could argue more. Had he touched an exposed nerve?

Whitney stood in the lobby, waiting for the other women. She wasn't looking forward to the foray into town, especially if Charlotte was going. Whitney had known more than her share of Charlotte's type growing up but she refused to revert back to that timid, sensitive girl who had hidden behind her weight. She'd worked too hard to let the Charlottes of the world control her life anymore.

She clutched her purse. The money Tanner had given her was inside. He'd paid enough attention to her that he'd noticed her clothes? Had wondered about her curves? Heat filled her at the idea. But he'd said he wanted her to have something that fit her better. She looked at herself in the large mirror in the grand hallway. Did she have the confidence to wear a tight dress? Have him see her in it? She'd spent so many years covering up, could she let go enough to do that?

Soon she was in a limousine with Marie, Charlotte, Lucy, Ellen and Sue Ann, all of whom she had met at the pool. To Whitney's great distress, Charlotte took a seat next to her.

With her nose pointed down, Charlotte said as if they were new best friends, "So what brought you and Tanner together? You don't seem his type."

Marie came to her rescue. "How about a glass of champagne on our way to town?"

Whitney didn't normally drink much and certainly not in a limo. Still, she gratefully accepted Marie's offered glass of the bubbly liquid.

"So where did you meet Tanner?" Charlotte persisted.

Her tone was far too condescending for Whitney. In the past women like Charlotte had made her life miserable. Now it was happening again. Why she'd ever agreed to this weekend Whitney didn't know. It wouldn't be over soon enough to suit her. She took a sip of champagne in the hope it would fortify her. "We met in college."

Charlotte gave her a sly smile, as if she had set her trap. "Really? I knew Tanner in college as well. I don't remember you."

She wouldn't. People like Charlotte didn't notice people like her unless forced to.

"I was there nonetheless. We had a couple of undergrad classes together."

Thankfully Marie gained everyone's attention, wanting to know where they would like to shop. When Whitney voiced no opinion she said, "Whitney, is there someplace special you would like to go?"

"I've never been to Napa so I really can't say."

"Then is there something you're interested in shopping for?" Marie asked.

After her conversation with Tanner there was. "Yes, I need a new cocktail dress and I didn't have time to get one before I left San Francisco. Do you know of a good place to buy one?"

A large smile came to Marie's lips. "I know just the boutique." She picked up a phone attached to the side of the car and instructed the driver where to stop. "There's plenty of other places nearby for the rest of us to enjoy while you're getting your dress."

Minutes later they were stepping out of the car in front of a store with two windows on each side of a glass door. In one of the show spaces was a beautiful red dress. The bodice was seamed in panels so that it would fit tightly above the waist, while the skirt flared and flowed around the mannequin's legs. It was so unlike anything Whitney owned yet for some reason she wanted to surprise, even shock, Tanner. What was happening to her? All her life she'd been in the background, had worked hard to stay there, and yet everything about the dress screamed, *Notice me*.

"I can see the red dress has caught your attention. Let's go in and you can try it on." Marie all but pushed her into the store.

The other ladies, including Charlotte, headed down the sidewalk with a wave of their hands. One said, "We'll meet you in an hour at the café for tea."

A small bell tinkled as she and Marie entered the shop. A saleswoman greeted them. Marie wasted no time telling her that Whitney wanted to try on the dress in the window. Minutes later Whitney was standing in front of three mirrors, wondering who she was looking at.

"It's lovely on you." Marie's words were soft and reassuring.

Whitney moved from side to side, watching the folds of the dress sway around her legs. "You don't think it's too much?"

"No. Tanner won't know what's happened to him when he sees you."

Did she want that? They weren't lovers. She was looking for a woman for him, not *to be* his woman.

"Yes, and even better, it'll get Charlotte's goat."

Whitney gave Marie a sharp look. "Why?"

"Because she seems to think she has some claim on him."

Watching Marie's face closely, Whitney responded, "Tanner said she's engaged."

Marie curled her lip in distaste. "She is, but that doesn't seem to mean much to her. Max doesn't spend enough time with her to keep her happy so she goes after other people's husbands."

Had Charlotte gone after Malcolm?

Marie picked out a necklace with a small pearl on the end of a stand on the table near them. "Turn around," she ordered then fastened it on Whitney's neck. "I'd like to see her put in her place. You might just be the person to do that." Marie patted her shoulder. "Perfect. He'll never know what hit him."

Her? She'd never outshined someone like Charlotte. Cautiously Whitney asked, "If you don't mind me being nosy, if you feel that way about her, why is she here?"

"Because she's Max's latest young thing." Marie didn't sound at all pleased. "His wife, Margaret, was my best friend. She died of cancer a couple of years ago."

Whitney touched her arm. "I'm so sorry to hear that."

"Thank you. It was a dreadfully hard time on everyone. Enough of that. Let's get this dress paid for and go have tea." Marie started toward the desk.

Did Whitney dare buy the dress? Tanner's

comment about her clothing compelled her to say yes, but she sure didn't want Charlotte goading her into doing something to prove a point. But just this once it would be nice to indulge herself, wear something that made her feel confident, feminine.

"Okay."

It wasn't until she was taking the dress off and looked at the price tag that she almost fainted. It was half her house payment for a month. If she could just find the right woman for Tanner his fee would help her afford it. Even though she had his money in her purse, she wasn't about to use it. Only because of the idea that wearing the dress would give her enough poise to pull off the rest of the weekend and deal with Charlotte's barbs did Whitney have the courage to give the saleswoman her credit card.

She and Marie stepped out into the sunshine again. They gave her dress to the driver, who was waiting nearby, and started down the street. The honk of a car drew their attention. It was Tanner. He pulled into the nearest parking place and got out.

"What're you doing here? I thought you were playing golf." Whitney didn't take the time to examine the little skip of her heart at seeing him.

"Turns out I was odd man out and not needed for a foursome. I tried to catch you before you left but apparently you have your phone off, so I thought I'd drive in and find you. Maybe see if I could join you ladies for lunch."

"Sure. You're welcome," Marie said, then started down the street toward where the others sat on a patio of a café.

Whitney whispered, "So why are you really here?"

"I got to thinking it was unfair of me to throw you to the wolves by pressuring you into coming into town without me to run interference. So when I wasn't needed for golf I came to save you."

"Just like a knight of old," Whitney jested. In reality she found it rather sweet that he'd been anxious about her welfare. Or was he just afraid she might slip up and tell everyone she was his matchmaker? Despite his high-handed method of getting her to come with him, he seemed genuinely concerned for her. It made it hard not to like him.

"Are you making fun of me?"

"I would never do that," Whitney said with pretend sincerity and then followed Marie.

Tanner caught up with her. He took her hand and leaned in close. "We need to make this look good."

A tingle of pleasure rippled through her. Just having him near made her feel warmer than the day indicated. She had to get a handle on her reaction or she would soon be swooning over Tanner like she had in college. That was a stage in her life she wasn't returning to.

Minutes later they had taken a seat at the table on the patio with the other women.

"I don't know if I've ever had afternoon tea. I might do this again soon," Tanner remarked as he picked up a sandwich that almost disappeared between his large fingers.

"You don't know what you've been missing," Whitney said. "It's one of the most relaxing things I do for myself."

"You've had afternoon tea before?" Tanner sounded surprised. Did he think she wasn't interested in anything that cultured?

"Many times."

"I prefer other diversions," Charlotte purred, giving Tanner a speculative look.

He ignored Charlotte and said to Whitney, "I'm going to count on you taking me to your favorite place. My treat."

The look he gave her created a low glow in her. He was putting on a show for the women but she was still enjoying his attention, no matter what the reason.

Tanner was a perfect charmer during lunch. He spread his attention around each of the women, including Charlotte, but he made it clear Whitney was special. Where some men would have felt out of place as the only male at the meal, Tanner seemed to be enjoying himself.

When he wasn't eating, his arm remained across the back of her chair. That element of his personality Whitney had seen when they'd been in college was now very evident during the meal. Occasionally his thumb would drop down and brush her shoulder.

When she shuddered he leaned in too close and asked with his lips just touching her ear, "Are you cold?"

He knew full well she wasn't. If anything, she felt compelled to fan herself.

Tanner entertained with stories of his exploits during med school and shared one very poignant one about a patient. Whitney envied his ability to fit in wherever he was. He even paid for everyone's meal, stating, "That's what a gentleman does."

"So, Marie, what do you have planned for us this evening?" he asked as they were leaving the café.

"Tonight we're having a wine-and-cheese tasting at the winery, then taking a tour and ending with dinner in the wine cellar."

They had arrived at the limousine and the women started taking their seats. When Whitney ducked her head to get in Tanner said, "Aren't you going to ride back with me?"

He almost sounded hurt. "Uh, sure." Whitney joined him on the sidewalk again. They watched the limo move away from the curve.

"Do you need to get anything else while we're in town?" he asked.

"No, I'm good." She already had a stunning dress that Marie would take care of.

"Okay. Then how about a ride through the valley since you've never been to Napa? It's a beautiful day."

Secretly pleased, she admonished, "You know you don't have to entertain me. Don't you need to be hanging out with Malcolm and the other board members?"

"Nope. I have you here and I understand the need to appear ready to settle down, but I'm not going to pander to anyone for a job."

She was glad to hear that Tanner had a moral line that he wouldn't cross.

"Let's take that ride. Do you have a hat?"

"No, but I have a scarf." She gave him her best mischievous grin.

"We're going to find you a hat." He grabbed her hand and pulled her toward a boutique with hats in the window.

A few minutes later, they came out with her wearing a tangerine-colored wide-brimmed hat that was far more attention-getting than anything else she owned. But she loved it. Between it and the dress she was really stepping out of her comfort zone. Somehow Tanner was bringing out her inner diva.

"That color suits you," he said as they settled in the car.

"Thank you. You do know you don't have to compliment me when there's no one around to hear?"

"Has it occurred to you that I might like complimenting you?"

It hadn't, but she had to admit she liked the attention from him.

Over the next couple of hours they just drove at a peaceful speed along the main road through the center of the valley. The vineyards they passed were impeccably groomed and endless. Tanner pulled over at a little roadside stand and bought them bottled drinks.

"This is so beautiful." Whitney stood beside the car, looking off toward the east where the hills created one side of the valley.

Tanner leaned against the car and crossed his ankles. "I was impressed the first time I visited as well. It's like a little piece of France at your back door."

"I would love to visit France one day." Whitney took a sip of her cola.

"I think you would like it. I'd heard so much about Paris that I didn't believe it could live up to the hype, but it was everything I had expected and more."

"Do you travel a lot?" She couldn't help but look at him. Even his body movements captivated her. She was so on the road to trouble. Heart trouble.

"When I can. It takes some reconfiguring for me to get away from the hospital." He didn't sound disappointed, just resigned.

She met his gaze from under the brim of her hat. "So what about this weekend? Who's watching over everything?"

"I'm close enough to be there in an hour or so. I have good staff who will help out until I can get there."

Their lives were so different. Her career almost seemed frivolous compared to his yet he'd asked for her help. No matter what people did in life they wanted to share it with someone. The more she was around Tanner the more she could understand why he would be considered a catch.

But why was he so against a relationship that involved love? She had a feeling he had a lot stored up to give.

They were in the car again and Tanner was about to turn into the road to head back the way they had come when Whitney said, "Thank you for making the afternoon nice for me. It was sweet of you. I would have made it through tea by myself but it was good to have your support."

"You're welcome. If you have any issues with Charlotte, just let me know. Max will be here this evening and most of that will stop."

"Is she always so catty?"

He glanced at her. "Only when she can get away with it."

Whitney watched his capable hands on the wheel. He had nice hands. What would it be like to be intentionally touched by those fingers? That wasn't a safe subject. Charlotte was a more benign one. "She said she was at Berkeley at the same time we were."

"She was. We dated awhile in my senior year." He slowed and let a car go around them.

"I don't remember her."

"She transferred in." Tanner looked up into the rearview mirror.

So that was why she hadn't recognized her. Charlotte had been around during those years she hadn't seen much of Tanner.

They returned to the château around four that afternoon. Whitney pulled off her hat and shook out her hair as they walked toward the main entrance.

"You have beautiful hair. That chestnut color is so unusual."

"Thank you." Oh, yes, the man had charm. And was laying it on thickly.

He pushed a strand off her cheek. "You should wear it down more often."

If she let him keep this up he would have her in bed in the next fifteen minutes. "Tanner, I think we need to make a rule that you only touch me if it's necessary."

"Do I get to decide what's *necessary*?" He fingered her hair.

She stepped out of reach. "No, I think I should make that decision."

"What're you afraid of? That I'll uncover the true Whitney?" He waited for her to join him on the stairs.

Tanner was perceptive, she'd give him that. Was that the part of his character that made him such a good doctor? But he was her client and she had no intention of confessing any of her secrets.

CHAPTER FOUR

TANNER COULDN'T REMEMBER when he'd spent a more relaxing few hours with a woman. Whitney didn't need to be entertained. She seemed happy just being along. Few women he knew would have been glad to spend hours riding in a car. There was something reassuring about having Whitney in the seat next to him. It was an odd feeling. It was nothing like what he'd seen in his mother and father's relationship. He wasn't going into that emotional minefield. They had nothing to do with him and Whitney.

Now she was in the bath, preparing for the evening. He was confident from her no-nonsense personality that he wouldn't be left waiting long. After showering and shaving, he'd given the bathroom over to her. He had no idea what she planned to wear that evening but he was determined that his response would be positive, no matter what her attire.

There was a knock at the door. He opened it to find one of the bellboys.

"Mrs. Jarvis sent this up for Ms. Thomason." The young man handed Tanner a dress bag and was gone before Tanner had time to tip him.

Tanner closed the door. So had Whitney taken his suggestion and bought something for herself after all? He tapped on the bathroom door. "Marie has sent you something."

Whitney opened the door a crack. Her eyes widened when she saw the bag. "I forgot." She reached out and took the bag. "Thank you."

Seconds later Tanner was left looking at the panel of the door.

It had been twenty minutes since he'd heard anything coming from the bathroom. He checked his watch again. What was Whitney doing? They would be late if she didn't hurry up. He tapped on the door. "Is everything all right in there?"

A muffled sound reached his ears. That wasn't good.

The door barely opened. Her voice held a note of misery. "I can't zip my dress."

So that was what this was all about. "Step out here. I can help with that."

Tanner registered a flash of red as she came only far enough into the room to present him with her back. For a moment his focus was on nothing but the bare V of skin between the two sections of the zipper. Whitney wore no bra. He made himself swallow.

Stepping up to her, Tanner took the tiny pull of the zipper between two fingers. Why were his hands trembling? He'd seen many bare backs. The zipper didn't move when he tugged so he had to hold the material below it snugly, which brought his hand into contact with the curve of her back.

Tanner didn't miss the sharp intake of Whitney's breath. He was breathing harder as well. Getting hard. This simple action of closing a zip was turning into something personal, sensual. With the zip closed Tanner stepped away, shoving his hands into his pants pockets.

What was going on here? He had no particular interest in Whitney. Still, what he wouldn't have given to run the tip of a finger over the exposed creaminess of her back. Or to taste the ridge of her shoulder.

He cleared his throat and stepped back until the backs of his legs touched the bed.

"Thank you," she said as she turned.

That scalding desire Tanner had felt had been fading and now it ignited to explode throughout his body as he took in the full view of Whitney. Her dress was demure by most standards but sexy on Whitney. With a V neckline that only showed a suggestion of cleavage and a length that stopped at her knees, she looked amazing. Just as he had suspected, there were curves under those baggy clothes she usually wore.

Her hair flowed thick and free around her shoulders. Tanner fisted his hands in his pockets so he didn't reach out and grab a handful. "Whitney, you look lovely."

A shy smile covered rose-tinted lips. "Thank you. I'm ready when you are."

His desire intensified. He was ready all right, but not for something that involved anyone but them. He stepped closer to her. "We should be going or we'll be late. But before we do, I think we need to take care of something."

Whitney looked around the room as if she had forgotten something then back at him with a questioning look on her face.

"I know you said only when necessary but I might need to kiss you tonight in front of the others so I think we should practice. Get that first uncomfortable one out of the way. Settle the nerves, so to speak." Yeah, like that was going to happen. Nothing about the reaction she was creating in his body was settling.

"I guess we could do that…"

He found Whitney's lips with his.

They were soft and inviting. Plump and perfect. He pressed more firmly and a shudder went through her. Her fingers gripped his biceps yet she didn't return his kiss. Tanner pulled back and searched her face. Her eyes were wide and she looked dazed.

"It might be more believable if you kissed me back. Should I try again?" He waited. This he wouldn't push.

"Yes, please. I think it's necessary." Her lips hardly moved as the soft words left them.

Tanner chuckled softly. What little taste of Whitney he'd had made him want more. She lifted her mouth to his. This time he placed his hands on her waist and brought her against him. When her lips stirred, his heart drummed faster. Her hands tightened, fisting in his shirtsleeves.

The kiss was quickly moving away from practice to pleasure.

Seconds later, with one sharp movement Whitney broke away, turning her back to him. "I think that was enough practice. We should go." She picked up a shawl from the bed and draped it over her arm. The tightly controlled woman had returned.

Their simple kiss had left him rock hard. Staying where they were was more of what Tanner had in mind. But he was a man of his word. He'd promised not to ask her for anything physical. Their kisses might be considered bending the rule but he'd not push further. Nothing about Whitney struck him as someone who didn't invest emotionally and he certainly wasn't looking for anything that involved his heart.

"I guess we should." Even to his own ears he sounded disappointed.

Tanner's kisses had been sweet and nonthreatening yet they sure had rocked Whitney's world. Even now as they walked across the parking area toward the winery she still trembled. She'd been kissed before but none had been as divine as those Tanner had gifted her with. The problem now was that she wanted more, but she wouldn't let that happen.

She could be in trouble on so many levels. He was her client. He didn't believe in love. He was looking for a wife. She was nothing like what he wanted. He would break her heart. Of that she was confident. She had to get through this weekend and see to it that they returned to their business relationship.

When she stumbled, Tanner's hand was on her elbow to steady her instantly. "I'm sorry, Whitney. I promised nothing physical. I shouldn't have kissed you. It won't happen again. It'll be your call from now on."

Was that statement supposed to make her feel better? It sounded as if he regretted their kisses. Here she was trying to hold herself together while it hadn't had any effect on him. She couldn't have him thinking that she was some ninny who fell apart when a man kissed her.

Long ago she'd learned to cover disappointment and hurt. She'd just do it once more. "Not a problem. I won't hold it against you. It's no big deal."

Had she felt his fingers flinch?

"I'm glad you understand." His hand remained on her arm until they stepped in front of the tasting-room door to the winery. When he let go she felt the loss in more ways than one. That tentative friendship they were building had lost some stones.

"I hope I don't slip up and say anything wrong," she whispered.

"Don't worry about it. Let's just concentrate on having a nice evening."

Tanner seemed far too laid-back for someone who was worried about his friends finding out she was actually his matchmaker. She sure wished her nerves weren't jumping. If it was from Tanner's kisses or her worry over disappointing him, she couldn't say.

He held the large curved door open for her to enter. Inside, the lights were turned low, giving the stone-walled space a cozy feel. It reminded her of pictures of a French farmhouse. To one side there was a bar with a full wine rack behind it. To the other side was a small, tastefully arranged shop area where shelves held wine flutes, cork removers and other paraphernalia. An upright, glass-doored cooler containing small packages of meat and cheese was discreetly positioned in a corner.

Sharing the other half of the room was a grouping of café tables and chairs. Each table was covered in a bright yellow cloth with a white dahlia in a vase. They were a pop of sunlight in the otherwise dark area. Greenery and tiny lights were draped above the doors and along the shelves. Whitney was instantly charmed.

"I love this place." Whitney couldn't help but be impressed. She glanced at Tanner. He was giving her an indulgent look.

"Has anyone ever told you that you have a beautiful smile?"

"No."

He held her gaze as he said softly, "They should have because you do."

Tanner's voice vibrated through her. Had anyone ever looked at her like that before? Like she was the most special thing in the world?

"I think if you continue to look at me that way I'll forget my promises," he said quietly. "Maybe we should join the others? I've been told that the Garonne Winery has a remarkable white."

Whitney didn't drink much but she was in the mood to enjoy some wine with Tanner. She would *not* get any ideas where he was concerned. The only reason he was paying this much attention to her was because he was putting on a show. But that kiss had felt real. That moment just now had felt real too. She was going to enjoy this feeling while she could.

He took her hand and wrapped it around his elbow and they walked toward the others gathered near the bar.

Marie met them, her hands out in welcome and a wide smile on her face. "Whitney, you look wonderful. I knew that dress was just the thing for you." She regarded Tanner. "I hope you told her how beautiful she is."

He nodded. "I did."

"Did he?" Marie looked at her.

Whitney smiled up at Tanner. "He did. He was very complimentary."

Thankfully, Marie didn't waste any time directing them to the bar. "You must try the white."

"Tanner said it was good," Whitney remarked.

Marie smiled with obvious pride. "It's our first award winner."

"Then no wonder you're proud." Whitney watched as the middle-aged man behind the bar dressed in a white shirt, black vest and pants poured the liquid into a glass.

"I must check on our meal. The tour will begin in a few minutes," Marie said, and whirled away.

The bartender handed Tanner a tall fluted glass and he gave it to her, then took his own. He tapped his glass against hers. "To a nice weekend."

Their looks held as they took a sip of wine.

"Nice," Tanner said. "What did you think?"

"I'm not much of a wine connoisseur so I can't really say." Once again she was out of her element.

"That's okay. You either like it or not."

She paused a moment. Was he talking about more than wine? "I like it."

Tanner smiled. "Was that so hard?"

"No."

"Would you like a lesson on how to taste wine?" He made it sound like it was something intimate between them.

"I'm always willing to learn something new." Had she really said something that flirtatious?

Tanner's eyes darkened but his grin was an easy one. "That's good to know. Okay, let me show you. First, you look at it." He brought his glass up so that it caught the light. "Then swirl it gently so that you can get the bouquet." Tanner put his nose to the rim.

Whitney followed his lead, doing exactly as he did.

"Next you take a sip in your mouth and swish it around, letting each taste bud have its turn."

Whitney watched, enthralled, as Tanner's lips moved against the edge of the glass. Those same lips had just touched hers. She had tasted their fullness and she wanted more.

"Appreciate the richness of it. Then swallow."

She watched the long length of his neck as he drank. He was making the process a seduction. Heaven help her, he was a temptation she was having a hard time resisting. She no longer needed her wrap in the cool, dark room. It had turned far too warm for her. Tanner had an effect on her like no other male. He wasn't what she needed but she couldn't seem to stay away.

His gaze met hers. Tanner asked in a low raspy voice, "Do you still like it?"

He wasn't referring to the wine. The innuendo was clear. She licked her bottom lip.

Tanner's nostrils flared. He looked as if he might grab her. This time the kiss wouldn't be a practice one, she was sure.

The moment was shattered when Malcolm slapped him on the back. "Tanner, how're you doing this evening? We missed you on the course. I'd hoped we would get a chance to talk."

Tanner's attention went to Malcolm and that suited Whitney fine. She wasn't sure she could have handled the intensity she'd seen in Tanner's eyes if they had continued uninterrupted.

The two men talked about general hospital

business and Whitney stood by listening but not really understanding the nuances of the conversation. Still, she enjoyed the rumble of Tanner's voice as it became animated about an issue. She was content to just listen to him. Mercy, she had it bad. Just like trying to return a cork to a bottle once it was out, there was no going back. She was falling for Tanner.

Marie had just touched Malcolm's arm, reminding him it was time for the tour, when Charlotte, hanging on the arm of a distinguished-looking man with snow-white hair, entered the room. Everyone in the room looked in their direction. The atmosphere took on a tense air.

"Well, it looks like we can start now that all the guests are here." The distaste in Marie's voice was unmistakable.

"Yes, it's time," Malcolm said in a pacifying voice as he took her hand. "Ladies and gentlemen, I believe they're ready to show us the winery now."

As if on cue, a young man dressed identically to the bartender came to stand at Malcolm's side.

"Please follow me," the young man said as he opened a wrought-iron door and walked along a passage. Whitney, Tanner's hand at her elbow, followed the other members of their small group through the stone opening into a modernized cement-floored room with large aluminum vats.

The guide began telling them how the grapes were harvested and pressed. Charlotte and her partner, who Whitney hadn't been introduced to, came to stand beside her and Tanner. The entire time the guide was talking Charlotte was busy whispering in the man's ear and giggling. Once Whitney saw him give her butt a squeeze and was disgusted by the display. It was as if Charlotte wanted everyone to pay attention to them. A few times she noticed Tanner glancing in their direction. Did this show bother him as well? Was Charlotte putting it on for Tanner? As if he knew what she was thinking, his arm came around her waist and brought her close.

"Now, if you'll follow me," their guide announced, "we'll go into the cellar where the wine is stored in oak barrels to let time create our award-winning vintages."

They entered another room where barrel after wooden barrel were piled on top of each other in ranks. They were stacked well above Tanner's head.

Whitney pulled at her shawl, trying to bring it up over her bare shoulders as the coolness of the windowless wine cellar surrounded her. Tanner's fingertips brushed her arm. Why did she have to love his touch so much? The wrap was lifted off her. Seconds later, it came to rest across her shoulders.

"Thank you."

"You're welcome." His voice warmed her as much as the material around her.

They continued down the wide aisle until they came to an area where three formally dressed tables were set for dinner. A single candle flickered in the center of each.

"Everyone." Marie gained their attention. "This is where we'll be having dinner tonight.

"Charlotte and Max, you'll be at this table." She pointed to one to her right. "Ellen, you and Carlos will be joining them. Lucy and Rick, you'll be at this table with Whitney and Tanner." She touched the table closest to her. "Sue Ann and Russell, you'll join Malcolm and I here." She indicated the table off to the right.

Whitney couldn't deny she was relieved not to have to spend the entire dinner with Charlotte. The woman rubbed her up the wrong way for more than one reason. What Tanner had ever seen in her Whitney couldn't imagine.

Tanner held the chair for her to sit. His hand brushed her neck as he moved to take the chair at her left. A shiver of pleasure went through her. Had he done that on purpose? Her reaction to him was on overload tonight. The romantic setting must be getting to her.

A waitress came to stand beside the table and popped the cork off a bottle of red wine. She presented a glass to Tanner. He sipped and nodded. She then poured each person at the table a glass.

Whitney liked their tablemates, Lucy and Rick. She had gotten to know Lucy a little during the trip to town but found Rick an interesting yet bookwormish type. Their conversation was steady and often drew laughter. Whitney felt herself relaxing. Midway through the meal she'd forgotten all her worry over whether or not she might fit in.

"I can't believe I've found someone as interested as me in growing violets," Lucy commented.

"Just goes to show you never know about people until you get to know them," Tanner said as he looked at Whitney. "We always get surprised."

Was he talking people in general or her in particular? How had she surprised him? Why would he be interested enough to notice? After all, she was only his matchmaker.

"Yeah, and after this weekend I'd be surprised if I get that promotion as Director of Infectious Diseases," Rick said.

Lucy placed her hand over his. "Now, you don't know that."

"I just have a feeling," Rick said.

"What do you mean?" Tanner asked.

Rick lifted his glass. "I don't think you need to worry. You're the perfect person for the cardiothoracic department. It's just something Malcolm remarked that Max had said."

Tanner turned in Charlotte's direction. She was laughing loudly. "He does seem distracted."

"Don't give up hope yet, honey," Lucy encouraged.

Rick shrugged and took a sip of his wine. "Let's talk about something else."

By then the salad had been removed and the entrée of prime rib and roasted potatoes with green beans was placed in front of them. As they ate they discussed a recent movie.

Whitney enjoyed the delicious food too much. Tanner smiled at her as she put the last bite in her mouth. "Good?"

"Yes."

"I like a woman who enjoys eating." Tanner's attention returned to his plate.

A sick feeling formed in Whitney's stomach. Her fork hit the edge of the plate with a clink. Tanner glanced at her. His expression turned from one of happiness to distress. His hand took hers under the table and squeezed. "Did I say something wrong?"

He truly looked perplexed. Whitney felt sorry for him. "No. I'm fine." She made herself smile. Would she ever reach the point where she didn't think every remark regarding her and food was a negative one?

Minutes later the waitress removed their plates and brought another with chocolate à la mode on it. Whitney stuck the tines of her fork in it and put a bite in her mouth. The shot of chocolate tasted wonderful but she took no more of the dessert. She saw Tanner look at her uneaten sweet but he said nothing.

With dinner finished, Marie stood. "Before we all go on our separate ways for the evening I'd like to give you a little idea of what we have planned for tomorrow. First, we're going on a hot-air balloon ride. We'll have to be up before daylight but I promise it'll be worth it. If you haven't seen Napa from the sky you haven't seen Napa. Cars will be outside the main entrance to take you to the field at six thirty." Charlotte groaned loudly as Marie continued, "The rest of the day is yours. Dinner is at eight beside the pool. Casual dress is fine. Malcolm and I have enjoyed having you here."

She and Tanner said their good-evenings to Lucy and Rick then thanked Marie and Malcolm for the nice dinner. Tanner pushed the door of the cellar open for her to precede him out. It had turned dark. The moon was big and full against the night sky and the air was cool.

"The hot-air balloon ride sounds awesome. I've always thought they were so beautiful."

Whitney pulled the shawl up around her shoulders. Tanner helped her adjust it.

"It should be fun." Tanner's words didn't sound all that heartfelt. Whitney didn't have time to question him before he said, "It's a beautiful night. How about a walk?"

She wasn't sure she should take the chance on being alone with him on a moonlit night but after the meal she'd just eaten she could use some exercise. She wasn't looking forward to returning to the room where they would be closed up together. He had too much sex appeal to ignore. Feelings that had nothing to do with looking for a wife for him had crept in, feelings that would only break her heart in the long run if she were to let herself act on them. It might not be a safe idea but she agreed. "I guess so."

Tanner offered her his arm. She placed her fingers in the crook and he set a leisurely pace toward the rows of vines to the left of the winery. The paths between the rows were so well maintained the walking was easy.

The night was still enough for her to hear herself breathing. They had walked some distance away from the hotel when she said, "I love this. It makes you want to take off your shoes and run."

"Go ahead." Tanner's voice was as deep and smooth as the night.

Whitney glanced at him. Suddenly she felt

like doing just that. He made her feel special. She kicked off her shoes, grabbed a handful of her dress and ran. The soft dirt, still warm from the sun, surrounded her toes. She threw up her arms and twirled.

A deep chuckle filled the air, bringing her to a halt. She looked at Tanner.

"Don't stop on my account."

She studied him for a moment. He looked handsome and sturdy standing with his back to the moon as if he were a warrior of old. She wanted to reach out and take his smooth-shaven face in her hands and kiss him for all she was worth.

She didn't have to. He came to her, standing so close she could hear him breathe but he didn't touch her. "Whitney, I need to kiss you."

Needed to? Had anyone ever needed to kiss her? She stepped to him. His lips found hers. This was no practice kiss, this was a man wanting a woman and telling her so.

Tanner pulled her against him, lifting her until her toes barely met the ground. His tongue joined hers and danced a measure that Whitney recognized as theirs alone. She held on and took the spine-tingling, heart-revving and mind-blowing ride. Her arms circled his neck as her mouth begged in desperation for more. She clung to him.

Tanner broke away, inhaling before he took her lips again. This time his hands moved to cup her breasts. They tingled, became heavy. His arousal was evident between them. The pleasure of having Tanner touch her made her feel weak. She clung to him as if he were her lifeline.

In a low growl he said, "Let's go inside. I want you."

Whitney was tempted to throw caution away and act on the fiery emotions boiling within her. She'd had no business agreeing to a walk with Tanner. It was too romantic, too perfect, too much Tanner. He filled her thoughts, filled her days, and if this continued he would fill her heart. That would be a road to nothing but misery.

If she agreed to his request what would happen to her self-respect, her business? What would happen to what she wanted out of life? A husband who loved her. Someone who invested his life in hers, theirs. She wanted a loving marriage, something Tanner wasn't willing to give. What was between them would only be a weekend fling. That wasn't enough.

"I can't." She stepped back, her mind forcing her body to move away when it yearned to cling to him. "I need to go in by myself."

"Are you running, Whitney?"

She looked at him. He stood with his legs apart

and arms at his sides. "I guess you could call it that. I know when something isn't going to end well. We aren't meant for each other. We are looking for different things out of a relationship."

Tanner watched as Whitney became a shadow among the vines. He knew she was right. Heck, he wasn't even sure what she wanted was real. He'd seen his mother fawn over his father, but was that love or obsession? His father had certainly not cared for his mother in the same way. Was his son even capable of loving someone?

He followed Whitney at a distance, making sure she safely entered the front door of the château. Along the way he picked up her shoes. She had such tiny feet for a woman who had such a strong will.

Once again he was pushing when he'd said he wouldn't. He'd apologized to Whitney more than he had to anyone in his life and here he was needing to do it again.

He went to the library off the entrance hall and poured a drink. Taking a seat in a chair near a window, he nursed his drink, giving Whitney time to get ready for bed and for him to get his libido under control.

It was late when the sound of footsteps drew his mind away from the woman upstairs. He glanced behind him. Disappointment washed over him. It wasn't Whitney looking for him but Charlotte. He returned his attention to the window, hoping she hadn't seen him. Sadly, that wasn't the case.

"Why, Tanner, is that you? I thought you'd be upstairs with your plain little woman."

If his hackles hadn't already been up they would have stood on end at that remark. The need to defend Whitney ran hot and rapid through him. He made no attempt to keep the aversion out of his words. "You know, it's been a long time since it's been your business where I am or what I am doing."

"Or who you are doing, is my guess."

"Or that either. You've found who you want in Max. Leave me alone."

She sauntered toward him. "The question is, have you found what you want in Whitney?"

Had he? "That's between us. It has nothing to do with you."

Charlotte leaned toward him, giving him an impressive view of her full breasts. "You used to think I was pretty important."

"Those days are gone and I've moved on. Now, excuse me." He put his hands on her shoulders and pushed her away as he stood. "I have other people and things that interest me more now."

"Like that nondescript woman upstairs waiting patiently for your return."

What had he ever seen in her? "As a matter of fact, yes."

Charlotte stepped to him so fast he had no time to react. Her mouth found his. Forcing himself not to squeeze her waist to the point of pain, he set her away from him. "If you ever touch me again, I promise Max will learn in no uncertain terms what a witch you are." He didn't wait for her reaction.

When Tanner entered their bedroom Whitney was in the bed, asleep. One lone light near the sofa burned. On the couch was a pillow, sheet and blanket. Tanner looked longingly at the bed and the soft, warm woman in it. After muttering a few expletives that he was sure would make Whitney blush, he shook out the sheet and let it drop haphazardly over the sofa. By the size of the piece of furniture his feet were going to hang over one end. Removing his jacket and shirt, he threw them on a chair nearby. His hands went to his belt. Normally he slept in the raw but he would defer to Whitney's sensibilities and wear his underwear. She would just have to deal with them.

He was on the sofa, curled up the best he could, when a soft voice said, "Goodnight, Tanner."

Had she been watching him undress?

CHAPTER FIVE

WHITNEY LOOKED DOWN at Tanner sprawled across the sofa. He'd thrown the blanket off his chest. His head was on a too-small pillow and one leg rested along the back of the sofa. Despite the unusual position, he was snoring softly.

Their kiss in the vineyard had kept her awake into the early hours. The passion behind it still had her feeling fuzzy all over. She'd been kissed before but not with the magnitude of Tanner. It made her forget all her reasonable thoughts where he was concerned. For once in her life she understood that "heat of the moment" concept. Tanner, the cool night, the warmth of the earth beneath her feet, the yellow moon above had all conspired against her. She had to see that she didn't get into that position again.

She was thankful for the second of reality that had crept in, for she had no doubt she was on the fast track to heartache. She knew rejection too well. Most of her life had been that where men were concerned. As a chubby child, overweight teen and college student she'd always been picked on in some form. She wouldn't set herself up for disappointment. Anything she might feel for Tanner would turn into just that. Letting a simple kiss change her entire life was ridiculous. Only it hadn't been a *simple* kiss.

She'd known the second Tanner had entered the room. Her body vibrated with awareness when he was near. She probably should have let him know she wasn't asleep but instead she'd watched him remove his clothes. No doubt she had been invading his privacy but she'd been unable to help herself. Worse had been the urge to touch him. When she'd said goodnight she'd seen the small smile form on his lips. He must have liked the idea she'd been watching him. It had been an enticing show.

When the alarm had gone off she'd quickly turned it off. There had been no movement from Tanner's side of the room. She'd lain there listening to his soft snoring for a few minutes before she'd looked at the clock. They needed to get up and get moving. Marie would be expecting them.

Delaying no more, she reached out to touch Tanner then pulled her hand back. For just a second she wanted to admire him a little longer. His shoulders were wide and the muscles of his chest defined. He must work out when he could.

A smattering of hair surrounded each nipple before it formed a line down the middle of his belly to dip under the elastic band of his boxers. Tanner's manhood rose high beneath the material.

She sucked in a breath that sounded loud in the almost silent room. What would it be like to be loved by him?

Heaven.

In a raspy voice Tanner said, "When you stare at a man in the morning, you should be prepared for what happens."

He grabbed her hand and jerked her down to him. Whitney's hands came to rest on the warm skin of his chest. Tanner kissed her. A now familiar heat built low in her. Without thinking, she leaned in for more. Before she could register what was happening he'd pushed her away. She quickly moved to sit on the end of the sofa where his feet were. A foot brushed her back as he came to a seated position as well.

Whitney blurted, "I was only trying to wake you. It's almost time for us to be downstairs."

He didn't look at her as he snarled, "Then go get dressed. I'll do the same."

"Are you always this grumpy in the morning?" she asked.

"No, just mad at myself. Now, go."

Was he mad because he'd kissed her? Even though she shouldn't, she'd like more. She'd promised herself when she'd gone to bed that their kissing was done. All he'd had to do was pull her against him and she'd forgotten that promise. What had happened to her self-respect?

She felt his gaze on her as she crossed the floor to the bathroom. A few minutes later when she opened the door, Tanner stood there wearing only a pair of well-worn jeans. He pushed past her, brushing her shoulder with his bare chest. "I need to shave then we can go."

"I like the stubbly look on you."

Tanner stopped and turned to her as if she had said something of world importance. "Then I'll leave it." He went to a chair and snatched up a sky blue polo shirt, pulling it over his head. She hated to see all that gorgeous physique disappear.

"Ready?"

"Yes." He held the door as she entered the hall. Thankfully his mood had improved since he'd woken.

Minutes later they were joining the others as they climbed into the limousines waiting in front of the hotel. Whitney sat beside Tanner, close enough that she could feel the tension in his body. She wasn't vain enough to think it had anything to do with her, so what was wrong? True, she had led him on when she'd returned his kiss then ran, and again this morning, but he'd seemed to have forgiven her before they left their room. Yet now he was uptight again.

As she climbed out of the car, Tanner offered his hand and she accepted it. He didn't release it as they walked toward the six hot-air balloons waiting in a field.

"They're beautiful. I love the colors against the morning sky." Whitney couldn't contain her amazement and the excitement bubbling within her. When Tanner said nothing she glanced at him. His gaze was fixed on the balloons. "Don't you think so?"

"Uh, yeah."

A man greeted their group and gave each couple instructions on which balloon basket to climb into. Thankfully there was a stool she could use for help getting in the basket but she didn't need it. Strong, sure hands came around her waist. She glanced back to see Tanner standing behind her. He seemed to lift her with no real effort. He waited until she had swung her legs in and was standing before he climbed in himself.

Minutes later the pilot released the tether and the balloon lifted. She watched in fascination as the ground moved away from them as they floated into the blue morning sky. The other balloons slowly joined them. It was a sight to see. Two rainbow-colored balloons, two shaped like a sunflower, another like a bunch of grapes and theirs in a harlequin pattern all floated above the green valley lined with vineyards with mountains to one side. Picture-perfect. She closed her eyes and took a deep breath of the fresh air. This was turning into an amazing weekend.

She turned slightly, wanting to get Tanner's attention to point out something on the ground. One of his hands had a white-knuckled grip on a support while the other grasped the edge of the basket. His body was rigid and his face was pale. Compassion filled her. She diagnosed the problem right away. Tanner was afraid of heights. Knowing how proud he was and not wanting to embarrass him in front of the pilot, she shifted toward him and whispered, "You okay?"

"I'm fine."

That was a lie. "You don't like heights?"

He glared at her as if she had discovered a shameful secret. "No."

The word sounded forced. She placed her hand over his on the basket edge. "Do you mind if I stand close to you?"

Tanner barely nodded agreement.

"Look at that winery over there." Whitney pointed to one in the distance, hoping that would take his mind off how far up in the air they were. She continued to point out landmarks and Tanner slowly relaxed. He even made a comment or two about different views.

"Why didn't you say something? We didn't have to do this," she whispered, looking at him for an answer.

"I thought I could handle it."

She chuckled. "Stupid male ego." For the first time on the flight Tanner's eyes held no terror. He gave her a sickly grin but at least it was a step away from the grimace he'd been wearing.

"I guess you're right. Thanks for helping my ego remain intact, at least where the others are concerned. I may never recover my knighthood in your eyes, though."

"I wouldn't worry about that. Your knighthood is in good shape where I'm concerned." She'd seen the care he gave his patients. She'd also been protected and complimented by him. His armor was still shiny.

He whispered, "Even after last night?"

"Yes." What he didn't know was that, given a chance, she would have liked that kiss to happen all over again.

"I'm glad." He sounded truly relieved.

Too soon for Whitney they were back on the ground again. Tanner wasted no time in climbing out of the basket. He offered her his help. She didn't hesitated to place her hands on his shoulders and let him lift her. Swinging her legs out, she slid down Tanner's body.

He kissed her forehead. "Thank you."

Heat washed over her that had nothing to do with the sun. Tanner Locke had needed her. Not as a pretend girlfriend but as someone who understood and cared about him. Hadn't he had that before? Why wouldn't he want it all the time in his life? As they walked back to the limo her hand remained securely in his. She was going to enjoy the feel of him while she could.

On the ride back Tanner continued to hold her hand and the old confident Tanner had returned. He talked and laughed as they joined the others in the car. He continued to touch her as if she had become his lifeline on the balloon ride and he didn't want to let her go. The one time he did release her hand, his arm came up to rest on the seat behind her. For once she felt that the actions were genuine instead of for show.

Her feelings for him were getting the better of her. She wanted to shout, *No, no, no, you are headed for disaster*, but her body said, *Yes, yes, yes, I want more*. Her body was winning.

When their party once again stood in front of the château Marie announced, "There is a brunch set up in the library if you would like something to eat. The rest of the day is yours. Sleep, swim, golf, go into town. Do as you wish. Dinner is at eight."

Whitney said to Tanner as they trailed the others inside, "I'm not really hungry. I'm going up to check in with a few clients. Don't worry about me."

"If you don't mind, I'd like to come with you. I didn't get much sleep last night. I promise to be quiet while you work. We can eat later."

Guilt filled her. He probably hadn't got much rest because he'd been trying to fit his large frame on the small sofa. "I don't mind. It's your room too."

With a wry smile he said, "Thanks."

Had he not liked her statement? Did he want her to refer to it as their room?

They climbed the stairs and walked down the hall to their room with not a word between them. She hadn't meant to make him unhappy. The less restrained Tanner was fun. Cautiously she said, "Tanner?"

"Yeah?"

"Did I say something wrong?"

He stopped and faced her. "It's just that you're always putting walls up between us."

"Walls? What walls? The only one I know of is that you are my client."

Tanner looked around and then walked to the door to their room and opened it. She followed him in. He shut the door with quiet control. "What if I don't want to be your client anymore?" He focused on her as if her answer meant whether or not the world would come to an end for him.

"Then I'll be sorry to see your business go." And her contact with him.

His look was one of disbelief. "Just my business?"

"Tanner, I'm not very good with word games."

He stepped toward her. "I'm not playing a game. I want you. Badly. Haven't my kisses told you that?"

He wanted her? His kisses had made her know she wanted him. Didn't a man like Tanner just play with someone like her? "I guess so."

Tanner came toward her. One of his arms wrapped her waist, bringing her close but not so near she couldn't see his face. "How little experience have you had that you don't recognize when a man desires you? Can't survive an hour without touching you?"

She looked at the rug beneath their feet. "Truthfully, not much."

Her few times had been short and sweet. Steve had left her bed saying, "There's not enough room here for me to sleep well."

"May I show you how much I want you?" Tanner nibbled at her neck.

She turned, giving in to the divine pleasure. The mere idea of Tanner wanting her pushed every thought of self-preservation out of her mind. Just being desired by him was more than she'd ever dreamed of. "I guess so."

"'I guess so'?" he mumbled against her skin as he continued to leave little kisses across it. "I've had more encouraging invites."

"Then you might want to go and find them." She made an effort to leave his hold but he held her in place. "Or Charlotte."

He pulled back. There was a look of disbelief on his face. "I don't want them or Charlotte. I want *you*."

Tanner's gave her a gentle and chaste kiss on the lips. Then another. Another. He was testing and teaching at the same time. His lips brushed across hers until she couldn't help but rise on her toes, asking for more. When his mouth left hers she whimpered in disappointment. Eyes as dark as coffee studied her. There was a flare of light in them before both his arms circled her waist and jerked her against him. Tanner's mouth crushed hers.

Whitney's hands found a life of their own and pushed up his arms to circle his neck.

He didn't ask for entrance, his tongue took it. At first he teased until she joined him in the excitement of tasting, tempting and tantalizing. Whitney's heart thumped as her blood rushed to become a throbbing between her legs. She squirmed against him, unable to get close enough. Her fingers weaved through his silky hair, wanting to feel all of him. This was what she'd been wanting for days.

She had become someone she didn't recognize. Tanner made her feel special. Sensual. Confident. Wild.

Tanner's lips left hers and moved to the pulse point beneath her ear. His tongue flicked across it. She shuddered. He was jumbling her thoughts. They centered only on him. He held her mind and body in his control.

His hands moved up her sides to cup her breasts, gently fondling them. His fingers found a button of her shirt and opened it. He kissed the curve of a breast. She clung to his shoulders as her legs almost failed to hold her.

Tanner released another button, pushing her top away so that most of her bra was revealed. Fear drummed in her chest. She couldn't let him see more. Know. Her hands stopped his when they moved to the next button. "Close the curtains."

His head jerked up. "Why?"

"Tanner, I'm sorry. I don't think this is going to work." She didn't miss the flash of anger that entered his eyes before concern covered it.

He backed away and, taking her hand, he led her to the edge of the bed. Sitting, he pulled her down beside him. "Tell me."

Whitney looked down at his large feet and her smaller ones beside them. They were so different. She the blend-into-the-crowd person, and he the shining star. How could he comprehend the pain she'd known? "You wouldn't understand."

His thumb rubbed the back of her hand. "Try me."

She'd seen him with Mr. Wilcox. His compassion, empathy. Could he?

"Please tell me. I know you like me as much as I like you. We're friends, right?"

He was right. They had at least become that. "I was heavy. Fat."

Tanner waited, as if there was more.

"That's part of the reason you didn't see me when we were in college. I wasn't one of those thin pretty girls you hung out with. You might not be interested in me now if I hadn't lost weight."

He shifted away. "You really don't have a very high opinion of me or yourself, do you? Has it occurred to you that I might have grown up? Can see beyond a woman's looks? Appreciate her intelligence? And you, can't you see what you have accomplished, not only in losing weight but starting your own business? You have a heart for people. Mr. Wilcox saw that. Marie as well. Is there some reason you think me incapable of doing so too?"

Whitney's heart swelled. She couldn't believe it. Tanner sounded hurt. "I didn't mean—"

"If I wanted anyone in my bed I could have Charlotte. You're my choice."

"You have no idea what it means to me to have you say that. But, you know, I have stretch marks. I still sag in places."

He gave her an incredulous look. Taking both her hands in his, he leaned toward her. "I don't care about that stuff. I want you. Just the way you are. I'm not going to close the curtains. I'm not going to let you do it either. You trust me or you don't."

"I don't know…"

He brushed her hair back from her face and cupped a cheek. His gaze never left her face. "Honey, I don't care about who you were. All I care about is the desirable woman you are right now. You're not running me off. I'm staying right here." He stood and kicked off his shoes. Pulling his shirt over his head, he let it drop to the floor. On the bed again he lay back on the pillows and crossed his feet. He patted the space beside him. "When you decide you want me, I have a spot for you. I'd be glad to share my nap with you anytime you're ready."

Could she trust him? Expose her vulnerability? What would she miss if she didn't? Minutes later Whitney watched as the dark fans of his eyelashes rested against his cheeks. She was tired too. They'd had an early morning. Maybe if she just lay down for a minute next to him she could accept what he offered.

If she did trust Tanner, act on her need, would she regret it?

Tanner woke to a warm body curled against him. Whitney lay spooned along him. At least that was a step forward. Except for the time she'd remarked about his facial hair and the moment in the balloon, had she shown him any real attention? Her kisses told him otherwise but she fenced him off when she wasn't in his arms.

It had been her choice to lie next to him. Progress. Good progress.

He brought his free arm over her waist and shifted toward her. Even now his libido was stirring, just being this close to her.

Whitney let out a small sigh as she wiggled her behind. He was in real trouble now. With a resolve he hadn't known he had, Tanner closed his eyes and went back to sleep.

The movement of the bed brought him awake again. Whitney had rolled to face him. She slowly opened her eyes.

His gaze met her green, unsure one and saw the second she registered where she was. "Whitney, if you don't want me to take you here and now in broad daylight, I would get off this bed," he said in a soft but firm voice.

She blinked then her look returned to his clear and confident. Her hand came up to rest on his chest. "What if I do?"

Her touch almost scorched his skin. "I want to see all of you. Appreciate everything about you." She waited so long to respond he was afraid all his desires would be dashed.

"Okay," she said softly.

Tanner reached to undo the button he'd undone earlier. His fingers moved to the next one then the next until he could push the shirt away from her shoulders. Sitting up, she let him remove it. He held her gaze as he reached around her and flipped the hook to her no-frills bra open.

She slowly let the bra drop to the floor.

"Now lie back so I can take in your beauty."

Tanner held her uncertain look as Whitney slowly lowered her head to the pillow. His gaze left hers to take in the view of her plump and perfect breasts. He touched the tip of one and heard the intake of her breath. His eyes lifted to her face. With her mouth forming an O and her eyes wide in wonder, he was sure Whitney was the most astonishing creature he'd ever known. "I don't know what you were worried about. You're beautiful."

"Don't look too close."

"Aw, honey, too late for that." His hand cupped a globe and lifted it so that he could take the nipple into his mouth. As he sucked and swirled his tongue, hissing sounds came from Whitney.

He raised his head. Her eyes were closed and she bit part of her bottom lip.

"Whitney."

Her eyes gradually opened. "Yes?"

"Please don't abuse that beautiful lip of yours. I wish to kiss it." He claimed her mouth as he continued enjoying the feel of her breast. She returned his kisses. Her hands traveled over his back and shoulders as if she were hungry for him. He sure hoped so because he was starting to hurt for her. "I need to see all of you."

The worried look returned to her eyes and she started to turn away from him. Tanner kissed her, stopping the move.

"You must think I'm some prima donna who is so uptight she can't let go enough to let a man see her."

"You certainly have nothing to be ashamed of. Don't you remember me being scared of heights this morning? You came to my rescue. I'm just coming to yours this time."

She looked at him then. "But you got in the balloon despite your fear."

"And aren't you here despite yours?"

She nodded.

He ran his hand along her ribs to her waist. "How about we do this together?" Tanner stood beside the bed and offered her a hand. Much to his delight, she didn't hesitate in taking it. As she stood he couldn't help but enjoy watching her ripe breasts moving freely. His gaze found hers. Whitney was waiting for his reaction. He took her hand and placed it on his length. "See what you're doing to me?"

A spark he'd only seen in her eyes when she was emotional about something he had said or done flared just before she stroked him softly.

Tanner stepped out of her reach. "Any more of that and I won't wait until you take off your clothes, I'll tear them off."

Her smile was a wicked one. His Whitney was gaining confidence. His Whitney? The idea was far more possessive than he liked.

With her hands at the button at her waist she said, "On three."

Tanner forgot all about his mental slip and watched her undo the button. He soon caught up with her actions and they both stood naked before each other.

"Whitney, look at me." He chuckled. "Not that part of me. Up here."

Her gaze rose to meet his. A delightful rosy color covered her cheeks.

"That wasn't so bad, was it?"

"No-o-o..."

"Now I'm going to look at you and you can look at me."

Whitney couldn't believe she was standing in a room naked before Tanner with the sun streaming through the windows. What had happened to her? Who was she becoming?

Trembling, she watched as Tanner's gaze left hers and started downward. His nose flared and his eyes darkened. With an index finger he lightly traced the curve of her hip. Almost reverently he said, "I see nothing that should be hidden."

Relief, desire and an emotion that went deeper filled Whitney. For once in her life she felt she measured up. She took that confidence and found her own pleasure. Studying Tanner's shoulders and chest, she let her look rove over his flat stomach to his slim hips. He stood strong and proud, and incredibly large. Her gaze continued down to his feet, where he wiggled his toes.

She looked at him and smiled. "There was a time I thought you had no sense of humor."

"I'm a man of many surprises. And right now I'm going to show you some of those." He grabbed her and lifted her onto the bed. "And I plan to touch every part of that lovely body."

"Shouldn't we get under the covers?"

"No. I want to experience you. Watch the light dance off your skin. See your expression as you climax."

"Oh!"

"I bet we can do much better than 'oh'…" Tanner kissed her deeply as his fingers caressed her breasts. Heat began to build. Involuntarily she flexed her hips.

Tanner continued to kiss her as his hand left her breast and moved to lie over her belly. Slowly, his hand lowered to her curls and over them. His lips moved over her cheek to nip at her earlobe. He whispered, "Open for me, beautiful Whitney."

She released the tension from her legs, let them part. Tanner didn't pause before he cupped her hot, throbbing center. A finger teased her, then pushed inside. Whitney bucked.

"Easy," Tanner said, then he kissed her and his tongue started making the same erotic motions as his finger.

Whitney sucked in a tight breath and arched her back. Tanner thrust his finger again and she wriggled against it. She squeezed her eyes closed. A heated swirl grew deep in her, built and curled into itself, tightening, growing. Tanner eased deeper and the spring popped. Pleasure flowed throughout her. She rode a sunbeam down with a sigh.

Her eyes opened and she looked into Tanner's grinning face. He teased, "You liked that, didn't you?"

"Mmm…"

"I think you'll like this as well." Tanner reached for the foil packet he'd pulled out of his wallet earlier and placed on the bedside table. He opened it and covered himself before he leaned over her, supporting his torso with his hands. Hers came to his shoulders. He kissed one of her breasts and she felt the pull deep in her center. Moving to the other nipple, he gave it the same attention. His length nudged her opening. He flexed his hips forward and Whitney allowed him passage. Tanner eased into her. With each push-pull her fingers contracted into the muscles of his upper back. With one final plunge he filled her completely.

After a few seconds Tanner withdrew and then pushed forward, then followed the same pattern until that fist of heat started tightening again. She squirmed, wanting more of him. He kissed her then pushed hard and sent her soaring once again. Whitney was on her way down when Tanner made three quick forward motions. He groaned deep in his throat then collapsed beside her.

His arm circled her waist, pulling her to him.

He brushed the hair from her forehead. "That was far better than 'oh.'"

Whitney smiled. It was. Much better.

CHAPTER SIX

TANNER POPPED ANOTHER grape into his mouth and watched as Whitney bit into a cube of yellow cheese.

He wasn't by a long shot inexperienced where women were concerned, but he'd never enjoyed giving or watching a woman receive pleasure as much as he had with Whitney. She was so responsive to his touch. To his amazement he'd appreciated her to the point of pain. He wasn't used to that kind of connection. What was she doing to him?

She had crawled under the sheets as soon as she could, saying she was cold. When he'd gone to the bathroom she'd pulled on his shirt. Why was she so uptight about her body? What had happened to her? No one was perfect. Where had she gotten the idea he was only interested in looks? He certainly hadn't been focused on that aspect when he'd listed what he wanted in a wife.

He looked at Whitney. Wife? What kind would

she make? She'd certainly represented herself well this weekend. He already knew she had a kind heart. Did she like kids?

"Do you want children?"

She gave him a quizzical look. "Yeah, why?"

"Just wondering." This wasn't a discussion they needed to get into right now. She'd been so unsure of their attraction he didn't want her to backslide to that point again.

He sat up. "As much as I hate it, I think we should make an appearance down by the pool."

Her face turned unsure.

"Something wrong? You didn't bring your suit?" He ran a finger over the top of her hand.

"I've got my suit." Whitney scooted off the bed.

"Then what's the problem?"

She stood beside the bed. "I just don't like wearing it."

"Why not? I bet you look cute in it." He liked the way she looked in his shirt.

"And I bet you need glasses."

He chuckled. Something he found he'd done more of around Whitney. "I'm a surgeon. Don't let the rumor I can't see get started."

A smile tugged at the corner of her mouth. "You go on without me."

"I don't think so." He leaned across the bed and reached out, letting the pad of his finger travel down the opening of the shirt. He reveled in her shiver. "Come on, for me." Tanner saw her indecision.

"And what're you going to do for me?" she came back in a saucy tone.

He wiggled his brows up and down. "What do you want?"

She looked at the ceiling, revealing her long creamy neck, then back at him. "I get to drive your car home."

"Done."

Whitney looked surprised. "I should have asked for something more."

He came to stand beside her. "Hey, I can count on one hand the number of times I've let someone drive my car. Three of those were my mechanic."

"The others?"

"My mother. My brother."

"Tell me about your mother." Whitney sat on the bed and patted the space beside her.

"Trying to stall about going to meet the others?"

"Maybe a little, but I do really want to know about your mother."

Tanner shifted around to sit beside her. He looked at the floor as he said, "She was a good mother. Did the usual things mothers do."

"No, tell me about her." Whitney leaned forward. "What does she like? Do? Her favorite things?"

His father, his father, his father. Tanner thought for a minute. "She likes sitcoms, pink lemonade, dressing up and going to the beach. But most of all she loved my father beyond reason. To the point it broke her heart."

Whitney's gaze was intent. "How's that?"

Tanner knew better than to start this conversation. He also knew Whitney wouldn't let it go. "She would do anything for him. Forgive him for anything, and he treated her like dirt. He had a traveling job that she hated. She desperately wanted him to stay at home. He refused. More than once I heard them fighting, her crying, and the next morning she was hugging and kissing him. She was always begging him to stay."

"That must have been hard on you."

"She just adored him. He could do no wrong. I've never understood why she stayed in the marriage. Let him treat her that way."

"She must have loved him deeply," Whitney said softly.

Tanner made a scoffing sound. "If that's love, I want none of it. Obsession was more like it. It wasn't healthy for her, or my brother and I. And my father didn't care one way or another." He could hear the anger building in his voice. "Look, that's enough on that subject. Let's go put in that appearance at the pool then we can find something else that we can do, just the two of us." He gave her a wolfish grin, took her hand and pulled her off the bed.

"Okay."

Despite him having seen all of her, she still went into the bathroom to change. When she returned she wore an orangey, flowy thing over her swimsuit. Her hair was pulled back at the nape of her neck. Going to the dresser nearby, she picked up the hat he'd bought her the day before in town.

He'd already put on his swim trunks and his polo shirt. "You ready?"

She nodded but there wasn't much enthusiasm in it.

Tanner reached out his hand and she placed hers in it. He pulled her to him and gave her a kiss. She had a smile on her face as they walked through the château. One that he knew he'd caused.

There was no one at the pool when they walked out of the hotel into the afternoon sunshine. Tanner not only heard Whitney's sigh of relief but saw her physically relax. He didn't mind them having the place to themselves, glad to have more time alone with her. His obsession with Whitney was starting to concern him. Was this how his mother had felt about his father?

No, no, no. He wouldn't care about anyone to that magnitude!

"I'm going in. Join me," Tanner said as he pulled his shirt over his head and threw it on a lounger.

"I think I'll sit in the sun for a few minutes. It feels good out here." Whitney took the lounger next to the one he'd tossed his shirt on. She lifted her feet and rested them on the cushion.

Whitney had pretty legs. Ones that had been wrapped around him only an hour ago. His body reacted to that thought. She'd already made it clear how she felt about public displays. He was going to make one of his own if she didn't get in the pool soon.

After swimming a few laps in the pool, he came to the edge where Whitney sat. Splashing water with accurate aim, he was rewarded with a yelp.

Whitney jerked forward and glared at him. "What do you think you're doing?"

Tanner grinned. "I'm lonely. Come in."

"After that I'd like to drown you!"

He pushed away from the side, backstroking to the middle of the pool. "Why don't you come in and try?"

Seconds later she stood, dropped her hat to the lounger, pulled the band from her hair, jerked the cover-up over her head and let it flutter to the chair. He liked this side of her. It reminded him of the Whitney he knew in bed.

He couldn't keep his eyes off her. Whitney wore a plain, navy one-piece suit that showed her curves to their best advantage. Her middle was charmingly rounded, which attested to the fact that she had once been heavy. It made her a real person instead of a stick figure.

There wasn't much time for him to admire her before she startled him by diving into the pool. Seconds later she was swimming toward him. He didn't move, thinking she was just swimming out to him. Instead, when she reached him she put a hand on his head and pushed him under the water.

Seconds later he came up, spluttering. "Hey, what was that for?"

"For splashing me." She had moved beyond his arm length.

He swam after her slowly, much as an animal sought its prey. "What if I dunk you?"

"I don't think you can so it doesn't matter." She moved farther away.

"Cocky, aren't you?"

She grinned. "You could call it that or maybe I'm just confident."

"I think I'll find out which." Tanner dove after her and to his surprise he came up empty-handed. As he surfaced he looked around. She was behind him in the deeper end of the pool.

Whitney just smiled. He'd be able to catch her against the wall. Diving again, he reached out and his hand skimmed one of her legs but couldn't hang on. Once again he came out of the water to glare at her. This time she was swimming toward the other end of the pool.

"I'd say *confident* was the word." She splashed toward him.

Now she was taunting him. He didn't know anyone who dared to do that. It seemed as if everything with Whitney was a new experience. This time he would have her. She was in the shallow end, easier to trap. As he came closer she moved to one side. He shifted to face her. She moved again. Tanner followed.

She giggled. It might have been the most pleasant sound he'd ever heard. They were playing like kids, something that he'd never seen his parents do. He laughed. "This time you're mine."

Whitney had a surprised look on her face for a second and he took advantage of that weakness to pounce. When he did she flipped onto her back and shoved a foot into his chest, pushing him away. Before he knew what had happened she was gone. Seconds later, her hand was on his head and he went under.

Tanner came up to her laughter and her taking a seat on the steps in the shallow end. "You've had enough?"

He swam to join her, sitting beside her. "You're good in the water."

"I've always liked it so when I decided to lose weight I started swimming for exercise. Even took a lifesaving course for the fun of it."

"I've been had."

"You started it." She pushed a handful of water toward him.

"I guess I did." This was nice. Just teasing each other. With his high-pressure job he didn't just have fun very often. "So what can I do to make it up to you?"

"Well, I'm already getting to drive your car, so how about you be my sex slave for a night?" A stricken look came over her face. "I'm sorry. I can't believe I said that."

Tanner shifted to one hip so he faced her. One hand went under the water to her calf then slid up her leg to her waist. Looking into her wide eyes, he said, "It would be my honor." His lips found hers.

The sound of someone clearing his throat broke them apart. It was Malcolm, standing at the other end of the pool. "I hate to interrupt, Tanner, but you and I haven't had much time to talk. I was wondering if we could do that now. Sorry, Whitney."

Tanner looked at her, unsure whether or not he wanted to leave her.

"Go on," she said quietly as her hand gently pushed against his chest. "This is what you came for. Wow him. I'll be fine. If I'm not here I'll be in the room when you get done."

It was nice to have someone being supportive of him, not just wanting something from him. He stood and climbed out of the pool. "I'll see you later then."

"Okay." She smiled. "I'm not going anywhere." She looked at Malcolm. "You know Tanner really is a great doctor."

Tanner looked down at her and winked. "Thank you." For some reason he walked away thinking he could conquer the world.

Whitney went back to the room after a brisk swim that ended when Charlotte showed up. She shouldn't let her affect her life but Whitney was in a good mood and the woman would poison it. She'd just as soon read as spend time in Charlotte's presence. Sitting in the corner of the sofa with a book in her hand, Whitney was surprised when Tanner returned and came straight to her, giving her a kiss. Demonstrative actions from a man were something she wasn't used to. She rather liked them coming from Tanner.

When he pulled back and sat beside her she said, "That must have been a good meeting."

"Yes, it was. Malcolm said the board was

pleased with my work. He and Marie really like you."

"I'm glad I could help." She just hated that they were not being truthful about their relationship. Even more, she wished it was true. She knew better than to let that happen yet she'd done it.

"How about we celebrate?"

"How're we going to do that? We're supposed to be at dinner in a couple of hours."

Tanner gave her a wicked grin. "I have a few ideas." He leaned toward her again. "To start how about we get it on here on the sofa?" He kissed her and his hand ran up her leg and under the sundress she was wearing. "Then we move to the floor."

"Floor?"

He nibbled behind her ear. "You can be on top if you want."

A flash of heat went through Whitney at the thought.

Boldly cupping her breast, Tanner said next to her lips in a voice that had turned rough with desire, "Then it'll be time for us to shower for dinner. I'll be glad to scrub your back."

Tanner took Whitney's hand and held it as they waited to fill their plates at the buffet dinner arranged in the grassy area surrounding the pool. She'd picked out a flowing blue-and-gray dress to wear and Tanner didn't even think to complain. He knew well what was under it. A satisfied smile he couldn't control came to his lips. They had celebrated just as he had suggested, to the point of exhaustion. Still he looked forward to taking her to bed later that night. Whitney was weaving a web around him that he wasn't sure he could find a way out of.

With plates filled, they were on their way to a table when his cell phone rang.

"I'll take that," Whitney said, reaching for his plate, "while you answer that."

Tanner gave her his plate and walked off so he could talk privately. "Locke."

"Williams here."

Tanner knew the minute he heard his physician assistant's voice that the call was important.

"We believe we have a heart for Mr. Wilcox," Williams said. "Won't know for sure for a few more hours but things look good. Thought you might want to do this one."

"I'll be there in an hour and a half. Keep me posted." Tanner rang off. As he walked back toward where Whitney was already sitting at a table, she turned and looked at him with concern.

She excused herself and met him. "Is everything okay?"

"No, but it will be, I hope. They think we have

a heart for Mr. Wilcox. I've got to go back to town."

"Of course you do. Let's say our goodbyes to Malcolm and Marie. I can be packed in five minutes."

That's one of the many things he liked about Whitney—she didn't require convincing that his work was important. She understood and supported it. Other women he had dated had resented his job when it had interrupted their plans. His mother had certainly resented his father's job.

Less than ten minutes later he and Whitney were packed and going out the door of their room. Tanner stopped and looked back at the bed.

"Did you forget something?" Whitney asked.

"No, I was just thinking I had other plans for tonight." For once he was the one hating the interruption.

Whitney turned an appealing deep shade of red and headed down the hall.

Marie saw to it that his car was waiting outside the front door. As a bellboy loaded their baggage Tanner said to Whitney, "I'm sorry but this time I think I should drive. I promise you next time. If one of us gets a ticket, I want it to be me."

"I understand."

They were pulling out onto the main road when Tanner's phone rang. "I've got to get this."

He put in his earbuds, not waiting for Whitney's response before he clicked the button.

Over the next few minutes he listened and gave instructions as they sped through the countryside and then onto the four-lane road back to San Francisco. He drove fast but not carelessly.

He rang off and glanced at Whitney. "I hope I'm not scaring you."

"No." And she appeared at ease.

"I hate it but I won't have time to take you home. I'll see that one of the security guards drives you."

"Would you mind if I stayed for the transplant? I think Mr. Wilcox needs someone in his corner. Maybe I could visit with him before he goes in."

Tanner glanced at her. "I think he'd like that."

A mile farther on his phone rang again and he spent the rest of the time on it with his team. Almost to the minute of the time he'd said he would arrive he eased into his parking space beneath the hospital. Whitney didn't wait on him to come around and open her door. She was at the trunk when he opened it to remove her bags.

"I'll put these in my office so that you can get them before you go home. I won't be leaving the hospital until I know that Mr. Wilcox is stable."

"I understand."

She walked beside him as they took the elevator up from the parking garage. They entered the hospital through a door that required him to swipe a card for it to open and rode another elevator up to the fifth floor. There they went down a couple of hallways and arrived at his office. Whitney waited outside as he set her bags inside the door and grabbed his lab coat.

"Now we'll go see Mr. Wilcox. He'll be in his room for a little while longer. I'll need to examine him then you may visit until I send someone to bring him to surgery."

"Will he be awake or will he have already taken some presurgery medicine?"

"He might be groggy from premeds but he should be awake enough to know who you are." Tanner started down the hall at a brisk pace. The retrieval team was on their way to get the heart. The clock was already ticking.

"Either way, I'll stay with him." Whitney hurried along beside him.

Soon they turned a corner and Tanner scanned his card again. Double doors opened. She followed him to the door of Mr. Wilcox's room. Tanner donned a mask and pulled his stethoscope from his pocket. Without looking at her or saying anything, he entered the room and closed the door. Now wasn't the time to think about what was happening between him and Whitney. He had a life to save.

Whitney was leaning against the wall opposite the room when he came out. He pulled off the mask and dropped it into a garbage can. "You can go in now. I told him I had brought someone to keep him company. I've got to go."

"I know."

He hated to leave her this way but if he kissed her... His focus had to remain on what was going to happen over the next few hours.

Whitney watched Tanner's long stride toward the double doors. He was a man on a mission. His shoulders were broad enough to carry the world. And he was about to do so with Mr. Wilcox's life. What would it be like to have Tanner watching over her with such single-mindedness?

They had shared far more than she had ever expected or anticipated. Tanner had opened up to her about his past. She was confident he didn't make a habit of telling people about his parents. Whitney felt honored he trusted her that much. No wonder Tanner felt the way he did about relationships. He'd never seen a healthy one up close.

But she knew what one looked like and that's what she wanted. To love and be loved. To have that closeness that came from understanding and caring. They were fundamentally different. Tanner wanted a business deal and she wanted happily-ever-after.

Whitney put on a mask then knocked lightly on Mr. Wilcox's door. Unsure if he was strong enough to call to her to come in, Whitney pushed the door open slightly. The lights were low in the room and the only sound came from the oxygen machine. Mr. Wilcox's eyes were closed. Maybe this wasn't such a good idea. She started to back out the door.

"Come in, young lady. It's nice to see you again."

Whitney smiled and said softly, "It's nice to see you too." She entered and closed the door before going to his bedside. She stood so he could see her without straining his neck. "I hear you have a big evening planned."

"That's what they're telling me. What brings you around at this time of night and on a weekend?"

"I was with Dr. Locke when he got the call about your heart." That made it sound like she and Tanner were a couple. That was the furthest thing from the truth. They'd enjoyed each other's bodies but there was no emotional attachment. "I thought you might like some company while you're waiting to go to the operating room."

"That's mighty nice of you. Pull up a chair."

Whitney tugged one of the bulky chairs around so she faced Mr. Wilcox and sat.

"So what were you and Dr. Locke doing this evening that I interrupted?"

Whitney was glad for the dim light to cover her blush. Making love everywhere they could. She couldn't say that. Making love? That's what she had been doing. Emotion was involved on her side. She was in love with Tanner. In love with a man who had no desire to love or be loved. She'd known better but there it was.

Whitney finally managed to get out, "We were in Napa for the weekend." One she would never forget.

"I'm sorry that I messed it up."

"Hey, getting a new heart is a big deal. Well worth messing a weekend up for."

"You're sweet. You remind me of my Milly. She always thought of others first. If she was here she would be holding my hand, telling me everything was going to be all right. She always saw the good side to everything."

"She sounds like a great person."

"She was." He said it as if he were thinking back over the years.

"Would you like me to hold your hand?" Whitney asked.

"That would be nice. I know it isn't very macho, but I'm a little scared."

Whitney pulled the chair closer to the bed. She took the thin hand of her new friend and held it gently. "That's understandable."

Half an hour later a nurse came in and flipped

on the overhead lights. "Mr. Wilcox, Dr. Locke is ready for you in the OR."

Whitney stood and pushed the chair away from the bed. "I'm going to say bye now. I'll wait around and see how you're doing. I'll be by to visit again soon." She leaned over and gave the man a kiss on the forehead.

"And I'm going to look forward to dancing at your wedding."

That was an odd thing for him to say, especially since she'd said nothing about getting married, but she didn't question his statement. Maybe his mind was fuzzy.

The nurse gave her an odd look. "Dr. Locke said you could wait in the surgery waiting room on the first floor."

"Thank you," Whitney told the nurse. "See you soon, Mr. Wilcox."

Over the next few hours Whitney watched the weather channel on the TV in the waiting room, read a three-month-old magazine and dozed on and off, but otherwise remained anxious about what was happening in the operating room. She was concerned on two levels. Knowing what Mr. Wilcox meant to Tanner, she was sure he would take it hard if the transplant didn't go well. Then there was her fondness for the older man as well. With her nerves in a jumble, she also paced the room.

She'd been in the waiting room almost six hours when Tanner appeared at the door. He looked tired but it was wonderful to see him. He still wore his surgical cap and scrubs.

Whitney hurried toward him. "How's Mr. Wilcox?"

Tanner smiled. "He's in ICU and doing well."

Whitney hugged him and he returned it. "Now it's time for you to go home. I'll walk you to the front door and one of the security guys is going to drive you."

"What about you? You need to rest." Guilt washed over her. He'd had to sleep on the small sofa the night before, had been up early for the balloon ride and when he could have napped more they had been making love. Tanner had had little rest because of her.

He directed her toward the lobby door with his hand at her waist. "I'll be fine. I'm used to this."

The security man was waiting when they arrived. "What about my bags?"

"They're already in the van."

She grabbed his arm. "You'll let me know how Mr. Wilcox is doing?"

"I'll call you if there's any change," Tanner assured her. "Now go home and get some sleep." He gave her a hug and kissed her forehead.

By the time she was seated in the passenger seat of the hospital van Tanner had already disappeared. It was three in the morning and she paid little attention to what was going on around her on the way home. What had happened to her life? The one she understood? Tanner had entered it and spun it in a new direction. More than that, when he left, and he would, it would come crashing down. She was a woman in love who was destined for heartache.

Love. Heaven help her but she had stepped over the line. She had to stop this now. Next time she saw Tanner she would return his fee and give him the name of another matchmaker. She couldn't continue setting him up with other women. That would be more than her heart could take. Covering up her feelings would be impossible. If she told him now, maybe she would have a chance to recover, heal. But breaking it off would be the most painful thing she'd ever had to do.

It. There was no *it* between them. They'd just enjoyed sex as far as Tanner was concerned. What was there to break off? As far as he was concerned it would be no big deal while her heart would be crumbling.

Most of the day had come and gone when there was a knock on her front door. Whitney answered it to find Tanner standing there. Wearing the jeans and shirt he'd gone to the hospital in, he looked haggard.

"Hey," he said.

Concern gathered in her chest. "Is something wrong? Did something happen to Mr. Wilcox?"

"No, he's doing fine. Even asking when you're coming to see him again."

Relief filled her. So why was Tanner there? "That's good news."

"Can I come in?"

"Oh, yeah. Sure." She couldn't turn him away now. Moving out of the entrance, she allowed Tanner to step in. He continued into the living room. Whitney closed the door and joined him.

"You look like you should be at home, getting some rest. Can I get you a cup of coffee?"

"At this time of the day maybe a soda or an iced tea." He was looking around the room as if evaluating it.

She waited, unsure if he would appreciate her shabby-chic style.

"Nice place. Comfortable. Like you."

Whitney wasn't sure that was a compliment but it didn't matter. Tanner would be gone from her life soon. "Thanks. I do have some iced tea made. Have a seat and I'll get a glass for you."

Gone only minutes, she returned to find Tanner with his head resting against the sofa back sound asleep. He looked out of place on the pink rose-printed fabric that covered the sofa, yet in an odd way he seemed to belong there as well. Pulling the thin white curtains over the windows to keep the sun from beaming in, she then took the crocheted throw, which her grandmother had made, off a nearby chair and covered him. The man had earned his rest.

She couldn't resist placing a kiss on his cheek. It was nice to have him near.

Tanner woke to the smell of something delicious. When was the last time he'd had a home-cooked meal? His mother used to prepare them in the hope his father would be home to eat them. Which had rarely happened.

Where was he? He looked at the blanket over him. *Whitney's*. The entire place reflected her. Simple, floral and comfy. All the things he hadn't had in his life until she'd come along.

Sitting up, he stretched, trying to remove the kink from his back. He'd been almost as surprised as her that he'd turned up on her doorstep. After leaving the hospital he'd just needed to see her. Whitney was like a balm to his tired spirit. Getting to his feet, he followed the smell down a hallway with a multitude of pictures on the wall. Many of them must be members of her family.

Humming, mixed with a song playing on the radio, came from the back of the house. He found

Whitney standing in front of the kitchen sink. Her back was to him. Once again she wore a flowing dress but it was belted at the middle, giving her shape. The kitchen was yellow and had bright modern pictures of roosters on the walls.

He leaned against the door frame and watched her for a minute. What would it be like to come home from a hard day to this scene? Somehow life would be better just being a part of it.

A faster song filled the air and Whitney swung her hips to the music. She moved to the stove and must have seen him out of the corner of her eye. She turned. "Hey. Feeling better?"

He started toward her. "A little, but I'll be a lot better after this." Tanner pulled her to him and his mouth found hers. She briefly returned his kiss then stepped back.

Had something changed between them?

"I need to check our supper. I thought you might be hungry."

Was that all there was to it? He wasn't buying trouble until it came. "It smells wonderful. I'm starving. I've not had anything since we left the château."

"Really? That's not good for you."

He liked her being concerned. "I'm used to it."

"I guess with your profession you would be, but that doesn't mean it's healthy."

"I'm sorry I had to dump you off with Security. I know that wasn't a very gentlemanly thing to do."

Whitney held up a hand. "Stop apologizing for that. You had a more important job to do. I'm not so incapable that I can't take care of myself."

She was so insecure about her body and so confident about other areas of her life. "Not everyone thinks that way."

"Then they're wrong. Have a seat." She indicated the table. "The lasagna is ready."

Tanner took a seat in front of a square wooden table already set with mismatched plates and crockery. A glass of iced tea was there as well.

Whitney brought a steaming hot casserole dish to the table and placed it on a hot pad in the middle. She went back to the stove and returned with a basket of bread. She was half seated when she jumped up. "I forgot the salads." She hurried to the refrigerator.

She'd done all of this for him. He'd never dated anyone who showed they cared by cooking a meal. "You have gone to too much trouble. We could have gone out."

"I like to cook and don't eat out much." She put the salads beside their plates and then picked up his dinner plate and started spooning a portion of lasagna onto it. Placing it in front of him, she then put a small amount on her own.

"Where did you learn to cook?" Tanner picked up his fork.

"From my mother and grandmother. They said a way to a man's heart is through their stomach. I don't know if that's true but my father and grandfather seem happy enough."

Tanner put a forkful of the lasagna into his mouth. "If what they eat is anything as good as this then no wonder they're happy. This is delicious."

"Thanks."

Tanner filled his mouth again. The lasagna might be the best he had ever tasted. Whitney offered him the bread basket and he took a piece. Even that he savored. After eating in silence for a few minutes he said, "So tell me how you happened to live in one of the 'painted ladies' on 'postcard row.' It suits you, but they don't come on the market often."

"This one didn't come on the market. It was my grandparents'. They're letting me slowly buy it. They wanted something smaller and moved to a retirement community. I begged them to let me buy it."

"I have a nondescript place that I almost never see. When I marry, the first thing my wife will have to do is find us somewhere to live." What had made him bring up that subject? He poked at his salad full of fresh vegetables.

"Uh, there's something I'd like to talk to you about."

He didn't like the sound of that. Suddenly his food wasn't as appetizing. "What's going on?"

"About this weekend, I, uh, don't think I can be your matchmaker any longer." She reached into her pocket and pulled out a check. Placing it on the table, she pushed it toward him.

"What's this?"

"It's your fee and the amount you gave me to buy something to wear. I bought the dress with my own money."

"I see." And he did. But he wanted to hear her admit it. "So you're running out on me."

"No." She looked at her plate instead of him. "It's just that I don't think I'm the right person to be doing your matchmaking."

"Probably not." Especially now that he had taken her to bed. And other places. He pushed the check back toward her. "I want you to keep this. You earned it."

Shock then hurt flickered over Whitney's face.

He reached for her hand but she put it in her lap. "I didn't mean it like that. I just meant that you had matched me and you helped me out this weekend. Nothing more."

"I don't want it." She acted as if he had offended her. Treated her as a woman for hire. Maybe in her mind he had. After all, he had promised he wouldn't turn the weekend into something physical and he'd broken that promise. His actions had put her in a vulnerable position both where her business was concerned and emotionally. He couldn't blame her for calling it quits between them. He didn't have to like it but he did understand.

Tanner reached for the check and shoved it in his pocket. "That's not all, is it?"

She didn't immediately answer. "Just that I don't expect anything from you. What happened between us was only because we were pretending to be a couple. I understand you're still looking for a wife."

When Whitney ran she did it in grand style.

He put his fork down and looked at her. "What if I want more to happen?"

"I don't think that's wise for either one of us. I'm not the affair type and that would only get in the way of you looking for the right wife." She refused to meet his look.

Tanner hated to admit it but she was right. He was already far too attached to her. "Then we part as friends?"

She glanced up at him. "Yes, of course." Her voice was a touch high. Was this more difficult for her than she was letting on?

"Well, then I guess I should be going. Thank

you for the nap and the meal." He scooted the chair back and stood.

She did as well. "I'll call you with a name of a matchmaker after I have spoken to her. She'll be in touch."

Whitney made it sound like a business deal was being concluded. He didn't like that at all. It was far too civilized a conversation for what they had shared. A business contract was what it had been but Tanner had started thinking of their relationship as more. He walked down the hall toward the front door. Unhappy with the arrangement, he still couldn't disagree with Whitney.

It troubled him how much he disliked the idea of not seeing her again. What really got to him was that she was nothing like what he was looking for in a woman. He'd even had a difficult time making her understand what type of marriage he wanted. If they continued, he would only be using her. He admired her too much for that.

He stopped at the door. Whitney had followed him. He turned to look at her. "I've enjoyed getting to know you. You're a special woman." Tanner kissed her on the cheek and forced himself to open the door and walk out.

CHAPTER SEVEN

IT HAD BEEN a week since Whitney had let Tanner walk out of her house. What she'd wanted to do was beg him to stay. Telling herself not to listen to her practical side, even though she'd made the right decision. But there was still a gnawing pain in her chest. He could be a difficult and demanding man, but she loved it when he let loose and laughed. They'd had fun together. In more ways than one.

Without question she had done what needed to be done. But that didn't mean she didn't miss him. The day after their meal together, she'd called a woman in town who was also a matchmaker. As a professional courtesy Whitney had asked her to take Tanner on. When the other woman found out who Tanner was she had been more than willing to have him as a client. Now indirectly Whitney would be setting him up on dates. She didn't want him dating anyone. What she wished for was for Tanner to want only her. Open his heart to her.

She was relieved and disappointed in equal measure when Tanner didn't answer his phone. She left the new matchmaker's number and told him that the woman would be in touch soon. Her heart felt a stab of pain when she thought of Tanner meeting matches. Touching another woman. Kissing her. Maybe even taking her to bed. After disconnecting the line, she sat looking out the window at nothing. It would have been nice to hear his voice. This was much more difficult than she'd thought it would be.

As the days passed it wasn't easy but she managed to live through them. Had she made the correct decision? Could there be another way?

She was a grown woman who knew what she'd been getting into when she'd agreed to spend the weekend with him. He hadn't coerced her into bed. She'd gone willingly. Even now, when she missed him with every fiber of her being, she didn't regret it.

Almost daily she called the hospital to check on Mr. Wilcox. All reports were positive. He was now out of the ICU and in a room. Whitney couldn't put off going to visit him any longer. She wouldn't hide just because she was afraid that she might run into Tanner. She'd learned long ago that if she wanted to be emotionally healthy she had to face her fears. She'd done that a number of times when she had been heavy. This situation was no different. The sad thing was that she was desperate to see Tanner, yet she was also dodging him.

At the hospital she made it to Mr. Wilcox's floor without any sign of Tanner. She asked directions at the nursing station to Mr. Wilcox's room. As she walked away one of the nurses said to another, "That's the woman Dr. Locke was with."

The other responded, "Not his usual type at all."

"You're right about that."

Whitney didn't like being talked about. Most of her life had been spent worrying about what others had been saying about her. Old habits died hard.

After her knock, she was surprised to hear a strong voice invite her in. She certainly didn't expect Mr. Wilcox to be sitting up in bed, watching TV and eating a meal. This didn't look like the same man she'd seen before the heart transplant. "Hey, Mr. Wilcox."

"Hello, young lady. It's so nice of you to come by."

Whitney stepped farther into the room. "Well, you look wonderful."

"I'm feeling grand except for a few aches and pains, but Doc Locke says those will go away soon."

Even the mention of Tanner's name made

Whitney's heart beat faster. "I'm glad to see it. I've been calling every day to check up on you. If I had known you would be doing so well I would have been here sooner."

"New ticker is doing the job. This day is my best day so far. So come in and tell me all the news."

Whitney had a moment of panic. Had Tanner told him about them? No, he wouldn't have done that. Mr. Wilcox must be using it as a figure of speech. She came to stand beside the bed. "What news would you like to know?"

"I'd like to know what you have done to put such a sour look on my doctor's face."

There it was. Could Tanner really have been so upset over them not seeing each other? "I don't know what you're talking about."

Mr. Wilcox studied her a moment. "I think you do but that isn't a nosy old man's business. If you won't talk about that then tell me about yourself. I know you went to Berkeley but tell me what else you do."

Mr. Wilcox had a way of getting her to talk that few people had managed. But Tanner had as well. She even told Mr. Wilcox she was a matchmaker.

"You think you could find someone for me?"

"I'll be glad to see what I can do."

There was a quick knock and the door opened.

Tanner came to an abrupt stop. Whitney's heart slammed against her chest wall. She'd stayed too long. She was unable to do anything more than sit in her chair and stare at him. Tanner was just as handsome and commanding as she remembered. Every fiber of her being ached to touch him. She'd missed him so.

"Whitney."

The sound of her name was so sweet coming off his lips. "Hi, Tanner." She pulled her gaze away from him and looked at Mr. Wilcox. "It's time for me to go."

Mr. Wilcox glanced from her to Tanner and back. Those old eyes missed nothing. "You will come back soon?"

Whitney put a hand on his arm. "You can count on it. I'm glad you're doing so well."

"I have to give part of that credit to Dr. Locke here. He's a great doctor."

"I know he is." She did. How could Tanner be anything but that? "Bye, now."

When she passed Tanner he reached out and caught her arm. His touch sent an electric shock though her. The simplest touch from him had her trembling. "Would you please wait for me in the hall until I'm done here? I won't be but a few minutes."

Whitney glanced at Mr. Wilcox. He was still watching them closely. She nodded to Tanner.

Minutes later Tanner joined her. He looked at her carefully. "How have you been?"

"Fine. And yourself?"

"Let's not talk here." He took her arm and led her around the corner to a small consulting room. Opening the door, he let her step in before he entered. The door closed.

"Tanner, I don't really have time—"

His hands cupped her face as his mouth captured the rest of her words. There was an edge of desperation to the kiss as his lips moved across hers. Yet he was holding back. His mouth left hers to run kisses over her cheek. "I've missed you."

Heaven help her, she craved him still. But they must be sensible. She gently pushed him away. "Tanner, we can't do this."

He let her go and moved away, giving her space, but still breathed deeply as if he was holding himself in check. "Forgive me. I couldn't help myself. Look, what I brought you in here for was to ask you if you would go out with me? I have two tickets to Jazz in the Park tomorrow night."

"Shouldn't you be taking one of your matches?"

"None of those have worked out. Besides, I enjoy your company. What do you say, Whitney? Go with me."

This time he was asking, not demanding, she do something with him. She knew better but she couldn't bring herself to turn him down. It didn't matter what the best thing to do was, she wanted to go. Wanted to spend time with Tanner. "What time should I expect you?"

A smile came to his lips. One that reached his eyes. He'd been worried she wouldn't go. "Seven. Don't eat dinner. I'll bring it." His phone buzzed. "I have to get this. I'll see you tomorrow night."

Whitney thought he might kiss her before he left and was disappointed when he didn't.

She had a date with Tanner. A real date.

Tanner had been out with a number of women but for some reason he was nervous about this date. Everything must be right. He enjoyed Whitney's company more than anyone's he'd ever known and he was going to do whatever it took to continue to see her, to have her in his life, permanently.

It had occurred to him that she was his match. The one he'd been looking for. She met all his criteria. Whitney enjoyed his company. She'd proven that over and over while they'd been in Napa. They were extremely compatible in bed. Which made her almost perfect. She wanted children, was a great cook, did well in social situations. What was not right about her? Their life together would be satisfying. He just needed to convince her of that.

He'd been planning to give her a little more time before he asked her out but, seeing her in Mr. Wilcox's room, he hadn't been able to wait. He'd missed her, longed for her. Before she'd been his matchmaker and now she wasn't. There was nothing stopping them from dating.

Now all he had to do was woo her, show her that they belonged together. Surely he could do that? Had that been what his mother had tried to do? But Tanner wasn't going to make the mistake his mother had. He wasn't going to fall in love. Somehow he and Whitney would make it work without that emotion.

The next afternoon after half an hour of indecision, Tanner settled on a light blue collared shirt and jeans with a navy jacket as his outfit for the evening. Dressy, yet casual. Before he left the hospital he made sure that he had two doctors taking his calls in case something came up. He didn't want any interruptions tonight.

He was at Whitney's promptly at seven in his freshly washed car. Why was he acting as if he were going to the prom? Because he wanted Whitney to see the possibilities between them.

Adjusting his collar for the third time and checking his hair in the mirror, Tanner climbed the steps to her front door carrying a small flowerpot. The lady at the flower shop had said she would love this one.

He rang the bell. No one came. Had Whitney forgotten? He pushed the button again. Waited. Relief washed over him when the knob turned and the door opened. Whitney looked amazing. She was dressed in a light pink sweater set and darker pink pants that skimmed her hips, and wore her hair down around her shoulders, and he'd never seen her look more beautiful.

"Wow."

She smiled. "Thanks. You look nice yourself."

He offered the potted plant in his hand. "I brought you a flower."

Whitney took it and gently touched one of the purple blooms. "It's beautiful. You remembered how much I like violets."

"I did." He'd won points.

"Come in while I find a home for this and get my purse."

Tanner would follow her anywhere. He'd never felt like this about a woman. Right now all he wanted to do was carry her upstairs to her bed. Hell, he'd settle for her sofa. But he wasn't going to do that. She deserved better than a rutting buck.

Instead of following her farther down the hall, he chose to remain near the door so he wouldn't be further tempted. She soon returned with purse in hand.

"I'm ready."

"Great. Let's go." He went out the door and waited on the steps as she locked up. Taking Whitney's elbow, he helped her down the steps. When she went to the passenger side of his car he redirected her to the driver's. "I promised you could drive. I thought you might like to tonight."

She grinned. "Really?"

He held the door open for her. "Really."

Whitney dropped her purse into the space behind her seat and climb in. She already had the car started before he was in his seat and buckled up. He groaned when she revved the motor.

She smiled. "This is going to be fun."

"You break it, you buy it, that's all I'm going to say."

"Oh, you're no fun." She pulled away from the curb.

Over the next few minutes Tanner sat back and enjoyed watching Whitney's facial expressions as she negotiated the narrow hilly streets of San Francisco in the powerful car. She was having fun. The evening was off to a good start.

When they were closer to the park he gave her directions about where to pull in and stop. He helped her out of the car and then went to the trunk and removed the picnic basket and blanket he had stored there.

"Nice. Fix that yourself?" Whitney asked.

He gave her a bashful look. "No, but I did call and order it."

She gave a bark of laughter. "If nothing else, you're honest."

"Yeah, about this, but I wasn't straight up with Malcolm and Marie. I plan to come clean the next time I see Malcolm."

They started toward the stage already set up in an open grassy area in the middle of the park. "Good. I felt bad about deceiving them."

They wouldn't be upset if he could tell them that he and Whitney really were a couple.

Finding a place where no one else would be sitting too close to them, he spread the blanket out. They took a seat on it. Opening the basket, Tanner unloaded the food. Tanner had requested raw vegetables with dip, ham and cheese rolls, fruit and wine.

"This is nice," Whitney said. "Who decided on the menu?"

"I did."

"Good choices." She bit into a carrot that she had pulled through vegetable dip.

More points.

They were just finishing their meal when the jazz band took the stage. After a couple of numbers Whitney shifted as if she couldn't get comfortable. Tanner moved so she could lean against him. He liked having her close.

"The music is wonderful. Thanks for inviting me," she said between songs.

"You're welcome."

She smelled of something fresh and natural. The temptation to kiss her neck was almost impossible to resist but he did.

For Tanner the concert was over too soon. He had to let go of Whitney.

He repacked the basket and she held it while he folded the blanket. When he was done he put it under one arm and took Whitney's hand. They followed the rest of the crowd toward the parking lot.

"Do you want to drive home?" Tanner asked as he stored the basket and blanket in the trunk of the car.

"No, I think I'll just enjoy the ride. You always seem to make it interesting." She settled into the passenger seat and laid her head back on the rest. Closing her eyes, she hummed a piece the band had played.

It was a sound he could get used to hearing all the time. Forty-five minutes later he said, "Whitney, you're home."

She rolled her head and looked at him. "I'm sorry. I went to sleep on you."

"No problem. I deal with people who are asleep all the time."

It took her a minute but she burst out laughing.

"You know, there was a time I thought you were so uptight that you had no idea what a joke was."

"I could say the same about you."

She sat up and gave him an indulgent look. "I've never been uptight in my life."

"If you say so."

Whitney laid her head back again. Speaking more to the night sky than him, she said, "You know, I had such a crush on you in college."

"You did?" It couldn't be anything like the one he had on her right now.

"I don't think you ever noticed me. You never even spoke to me but, man, I was crazy about you."

Tanner liked the softness of her voice in the night. "I'm flattered. I'm sorry that I didn't notice."

"Hey, don't feel bad. I don't think we would have liked each other then."

"Why is that?" He turned in the seat to see her clearer in the dim light from her porch.

Whitney shrugged. "I just think we both needed to grow up. I sure did. A few more life experiences make us see things differently."

"So what do you think of me now?" he asked quietly. His future depended on her answer.

"I…uh… I…like you. Far more than I would have in college. You're a good guy."

More points. This was going from a good night

to a great one. Was now the time to ask? With his chest tight with building hope, he said, "I've been thinking about this matchmaking stuff. You know, we're pretty good together. Great, in fact, I think. You're a good match for me. I don't want to look anymore. I'd like us to see where this will go."

She didn't say anything for so long Tanner was afraid he wasn't going to want to hear what she had to say when she did speak.

"Tanner, would you like to come in?"

Whitney knew what she was agreeing to. But she also knew what it was like not to have Tanner in her life. Just a week of it had been enough for her. She loved him. Maybe she could show him how to love. She wasn't going to let go of this opportunity. It might not come her way again.

Tanner was a good man. She'd seen that in his actions more than once. He had the ability to open his heart, she knew that with all of her own. She would find the key. There was no doubt that he was her perfect match as well.

They made it as far as her hallway where a small lamp burned before Tanner grabbed her. She let her purse fall as he nudged her back against the front door. "I've waited as long as I can." His mouth took hers in a kiss that said he wanted her here and now. Flexing his hips, he asked, "See what you do to me?"

Whitney's stomach fluttered in anticipation. She liked having that kind of power over him. She brought a leg up high along his as she kissed him deeply. This was where she belonged. The love would come.

Tanner stepped back and fumbled with the button of her slacks. When he couldn't release it she brushed his hand away. "Let me."

"I want you so badly I can't think." He nipped at her neck. Touching her everywhere.

This self-assured man was trembling with desire for her. It was a heady feeling. She flipped the button open and pushed her pants and panties to her feet, stepped out of them and kicked them away. Seconds later Tanner's jeans and underwear joined hers on the throw rug on the floor.

His hands skimmed up her thighs to grip her hips and lift her. "Put your legs around me."

Wrapping her arms around his neck, Whitney obeyed. His gaze held hers as he slowly lowered her until he filled her. Heat, raw and sharp, pooled at her center. Bracing her against the door, Tanner thrust and withdrew.

Whitney wiggled as the sensation rose, turning the heat into a burning flame. Her fingers bit into his shoulder muscles through the fabric of his shirt. She might die with pleasure. Tan-

ner plunged again as his mouth plundered hers.
The need grew, built on itself until she could
stand it no longer. She threw her head back and
screamed her ecstasy.

Tanner held her in place and drove into her
until he groaned his own release against her
neck.

He steadied her as her feet reached the floor
then swept her into his arms. "Bedroom."

"Upstairs, room on the right."

The morning sun woke Whitney. She stretched.
Her hand touched the space where Tanner had
slept. She smiled. He would return. So this was
how a woman well loved and in love felt.

Tanner did love her. He just didn't recognize it
for what it was. He would one day soon. He must.
She would show him what giving love instead
of demanding love was all about. With time he
would come to recognize the difference between
what his parents had had and what they had. She
couldn't believe any different.

At daylight he'd woken her and kissed her
thoroughly. "I have an early case. I'll see you
this evening."

Then he was gone. She was well aware that she
had to share him with his job but she would have
liked to wake up with him next to her. Maybe
tomorrow. Those were the type of demands she

couldn't make. He would balk at them immediately. Too clingy.

Whitney went through the day with a smile on her face. She forced herself to review some client information but her thoughts kept returning to Tanner.

That evening she was in the kitchen when the doorbell rang. Hurrying down the hall, she opened the door. Tanner waited there with a smile on his face and a bag in his hand. He stepped inside and closed the door before swooping her up into his arms. His lips found hers for a hungry kiss.

When he pulled away he said, "I've been looking forward to that all day."

"You get an A+ for greetings. You hungry?"

"Yeah. For you." He took her hand and led her upstairs.

Sometime later they came down again and went to the kitchen for dinner. Whitney could get used to this. While she placed the food on the table Tanner poured their drinks.

"How's Mr. Wilcox doing?" Whitney asked as they ate.

"I think I'll be able to send him home in a few days." Tanner cut his pork chop.

"That's great. I'm so happy for him. Did you know that he asked me to find him a match?"

Tanner looked at her. "Really?"

"He did."

"I hope he finds one as good as I have." Tanner grinned at her.

She liked being his match.

After cleaning the kitchen, they spent the rest of the evening watching TV, with Whitney curled up in Tanner's arms.

"I missed you," he said softy. "Please don't push me away again."

"And I missed you." She gave him a kiss.

The rest of the week continued much as the way that evening had gone. Tanner had to work late a couple of nights but Whitney was waiting on him with a smile and a warm meal when he came *home*.

The first night he'd been late she'd been wearing a long comfortable gown. When they'd made it upstairs to her bedroom, Tanner had pulled it off over her head and dropped it in the trash can.

"No more granny gowns. I'm going to buy you something that flatters that sexy body of yours."

Tanner's attention always made her feel sexy and appealing. For once in her life she was going to buy some skimpy lingerie.

After their first night back together Tanner had brought over a bag of his clothes. A few days later she'd cleaned out a drawer for him and given him space in the closet. Their relationship was moving fast but she hadn't been happier. Still, there was the nagging voice that whispered when she wasn't busy, *Will he ever say he loves you?* She pushed it away with, "I haven't said it either, but that doesn't mean it isn't true."

Friday evening they were eating Chinese take-out when Whitney said, "My grandfather has a birthday party Sunday afternoon. Would you like to come with me?"

"Sure. Why haven't you said something about it before now?"

She fiddled with her chopsticks. "I wasn't sure how you would feel about meeting my family so soon."

Tanner took her hand. "You and I are a team. I'd love to meet your family."

Team? She wanted him to see them as a couple but she'd settle for team right now. "Mom and Dad will be there. My sister and her family. Some cousins."

"I'm game," he said, and went back to eating.

Sunday morning he had to go to the hospital for an emergency. "I'll meet you at your grandparents'. Text me the address," Tanner said before he gave her a quick kiss goodbye.

She didn't like showing up at her grandparents' without Tanner, but he had said he would make it if he could. Even though they had only been together a week she felt lost without him.

Her heart swelled just knowing he came home to her every day.

They were just singing "Happy Birthday" when there was a knock on the door. One of her cousins answered and called her name.

"Yes."

"Your Tanner is here."

Her Tanner. Whitney liked the sound of that. She met him at the door. He put his arm around her waist and gave it a squeeze. "Sorry, I'm so late. Case was worse than I thought."

She smiled. "I understand."

"That's one of the many things I like about you, you always do." He gave her a quick kiss.

Why couldn't that *like* have been *love*? "Come meet my parents and grandparents."

"Lead the way."

CHAPTER EIGHT

TANNER WASN'T USED to all the noise and excitement, the laughter, of a big family get-together. He decided he liked it. What he remembered about family parties growing up was that they were elaborate and his mother had often ended up breaking down in tears because his father hadn't shown up. They had not been happy affairs.

Whitney took his hand and led him into a dining room where everyone was standing around a table. He stood behind her in the crowded space. Sitting at the end was a balding, white-haired man. Next to him was a woman of about the same age who was cutting cake and placing it on plates then handing them to a younger woman who added scoops of ice cream.

"Harold, how much ice cream do you want?" the woman asked.

"Six scoops," Whitney's grandfather said.

"Harold! Even on your birthday that is too much," the woman cutting the cake scolded.

Whitney's grandfather reached for her hand and kissed the back of it. "It's my birthday, sweetheart."

She turned and looked at the woman with the ice-cream scoop. "Make it three."

"That's what I wanted anyway." Whitney's grandfather grinned.

"They're my grandparents." Whitney pointed to the older couple. "That's my mom helping with the ice cream. I'll introduce you in a minute." The love Whitney had for them was evident in her voice.

Didn't she use that same note when she spoke to him? He would have to think about that later.

"Okay, now that the birthday boy has had his share, pass the cake and ice cream around," Whitney's grandmother instructed.

Everyone did as they were told except for a few of the young kids, who grabbed theirs and disappeared into another room or outside. Soon Whitney and he had their share. Most of the others left to sit elsewhere, leaving room at the table for them. Whitney headed toward her grandfather and took a seat near him. Tanner slid into the one beside her.

"Paps and Memaw, I'd like for you to meet Tanner Locke."

"Hello, sir. It's nice to meet you. And happy birthday," Tanner said to her grandfather.

The older man gave him a long look then said in a teasing tone, "You must be the guy who has put the smile on Whitney's face."

Tanner glanced at Whitney to find her blushing. "I hope so."

"And this is my mom, Delores. Where's Daddy?"

"He's outside, getting some more chairs," Delores answered.

As if he knew they were talking about him, a man with the same coloring as Whitney entered the room. "I gave the chairs to those out on the lawn."

Delores smiled at him. "Thanks, honey. What would I do without you? Have you met Whitney's friend?"

Tanner had every intention of being more than her friend but he would accept that title for now. He stood and offered his hand. "Hello, Mr. Thomason. Tanner Locke."

Her father accepted his hand. "Hi, Tanner. Joe Thomason. Nice to meet you."

"You too, sir."

"Joe, I saved you some cake and ice cream." Delores placed a plate in front of an empty chair across from Tanner.

Joe took the chair and smiled at his wife. "Thanks." He then turned to Tanner again. "Whitney says you're a heart surgeon. Interesting profession."

"I am. And most of the time it is." Tanner took a forkful of cake.

"It would be nice to have a doctor in the family." Joe grinned at his daughter.

"Daddy!" Whitney's voice went up an octave.

What would it be like to be a member of this family? Whitney must have really cast a spell over him. There was something rare in the air around these people, in the way they looked at one another and interacted. Rare at least in his experience. It made him want to be included. He couldn't remember that ever happening before.

When Whitney touched him he knew the feeling. Like on the balloon. Her smile alone made his life better. What was that element? Some would call it a connection. Others compatibility. Knowing Whitney, she would say it was love. Was it something he knew how to give? But if he did it would make him too vulnerable, weak like his mother.

His family, his mother and father's relationship had been so dysfunctional that he never thought of himself as wanting, or capable of being in, a loving unit. Whitney's family made him feel a little uncomfortable as well. As if he was looking in on something he had no knowledge of.

Over the next hour he met the rest of her relations, discussed baseball with her brother-in-law and listened to a conversation between her father and uncle about the best way to grill a chicken. When Whitney put her hand on his shoulder and said it was time to go, he had to admit he was ready. He wasn't sure he really fit in here.

They were inside saying their goodbyes when one of Whitney's nephews came running into the house. "There's something wrong with Papa Joe."

Whitney was ahead of Tanner as they rushed out of the house. Family members surrounded her father. She pushed through two of them to where he sat in one of the folding chairs. He was clutching his left arm.

"Michelle, get the baby aspirin." Whitney glanced at him. "He had some arrhythmia a few years back."

Tanner said to the man standing beside him, "Go to the convertible down there." He pointed down the street. "And bring me the black bag behind the seat." Tanner handed him his keys. "Everyone, please move back a step or two. Whitney, call 911. Even if this is arrhythmia he still needs to be checked out at the hospital."

Whitney pulled out her phone.

The man returned with the bag and Tanner located his stethoscope. "Mr. Thomason, I'm going to give you a listen. Just remain still. Everything is going to be fine. Whitney, I'm going to give you some information and I want you to tell the operator to relay it to the ambulance EMTs."

"I'm ready."

"Give them my name and tell them that I am on-site." She did as he requested while he listened to Mr. Thomason's heart. There was no question it was an arrhythmia issue. The man might require a procedure this time. "Tell them to patch you through to the EMTs."

Whitney relayed the message. Her voice didn't waver. She was a tough cookie even in an emergency.

Michelle returned with the aspirin in her hand and Mrs. Thomason on her heels.

Whitney said to Michelle, "Give three to Tanner."

She was even knowledgeable enough about her father's care to know what he needed in case of an emergency. Whitney took care of those she loved.

Tanner took the tablets from Michelle. "Mr. Thomason, I need you to chew these and swallow them. Make sure they go down."

"I'll get some water," someone said.

"No water. It could cause him to choke." Or if he required emergency surgery, he shouldn't have anything in his stomach.

"Joe, Joe, are you all right?" Mrs. Thomason

sobbed as she pushed through the group and rushed to Mr. Thomason.

"Michelle, take care of Mother," Whitney clipped.

Her sister did as Whitney said, putting her arm around her mother and pulling her away a few steps. "Mom, back up and let Tanner see about Daddy."

Tanner knew the answer to the question before he asked but he had to anyway. "Mr. Thomason, are you on any medication?"

"He is. The information is in my purse. I'll get it," Mrs. Thomason said. She pulled away from Michelle's arm and headed for the house.

"Tanner, the EMTs are on the line," Whitney said from close beside him.

"Good. Tell them the patient is responsive. Three eighty-one-milligram aspirin given." He waited until Whitney had repeated his words. "Heart rate one hundred and sixty-seven. BP one-eight-four over ninety. Respirations forty-five." He pressed Mr. Thomason's index fingernail while she spoke. "Little discoloration of nail."

Whitney repeated the information.

Her mother returned with the medication list and handed it to him. He reviewed it then passed it along to Whitney. "Let the EMTs know. If you can't pronounce it, spell it out."

Tanner did another round of vitals as Whitney read out the medicine names and dosages to the EMTs. Mr. Thomason appeared stable but Tanner still wouldn't be comfortable until he was at the hospital and some tests were run.

The sound of the siren from the approaching ambulance soon filled the air. Tanner looked up and scanned the concerned family group around him. "I need everyone to move way back. Give the EMTs room to work." Thankfully everyone did as he asked.

Minutes later he spoke to one of the EMTs then let them do what they were well trained to do. After they had Mr. Thomason in the ambulance, Tanner conferred with the ER doctor who would be accepting his patient at the hospital. Soon Mr. Thomason was on his way. Tanner put his supplies back in his bag and found Whitney with her mother.

"I'm going to drive Mother to the hospital," Whitney said.

She really had been cool during an emergency. Many people would have fallen apart if a family member had been in trouble. Whitney had followed his directions to the letter without any questions. She was someone he could depend on during a crisis.

"Why don't I drive you both? We can come back to get my car later," Tanner offered.

Whitney gave him a grateful look that included something he wasn't sure he was willing to put a name to.

"Thank you."

Three hours later, Whitney was standing in the hospital at the foot of her father's bed. He had an oxygen cannula under his nose and had an IV in his arm but otherwise looked no worse for the scare he had put his family through. A monitor on a pole nearby continually checked his heart rate.

"I knew you bringing home a doctor was going to be a benefit," her father said with a wink.

Whitney was just glad Tanner had stepped out to speak to her father's cardiologist and hadn't heard that statement.

"I don't like Tanner because he's a doctor, Dad. He's fun to be around, nice, caring and good to me."

Her father looked at her for a moment. "Sounds like a woman in love to me."

She was. Deeply. "There's a lot to love about him."

Her father grinned as he looked over her shoulder.

Whitney turned to find Tanner standing there. Had he heard what she had said? Would he run now, knowing how she felt? She tried to read

Tanner's face but there was no indication he had heard her. If she did tell him how she felt, would he even give them a chance?

She'd had no doubt that he was a thorough doctor and a compassionate one. With Mr. Wilcox she had seen some of those attributes but today with her father she'd seen firsthand how he could command a difficult situation. He had been magnificent. Someone she could lean on in a time of trouble.

Tanner came to stand beside her. "You're all set, Mr. Thomason. I'll be in to check on you in the morning. If you need anything, just ask."

"Thanks for your help today. I don't usually make such a scene when my daughter brings home a man for the first time."

Tanner grinned. "I'm glad to know I'm special." He looked at Whitney's mother. "Delores, are you sure you're going to be okay here tonight? Have everything you need?"

"I'll be just fine. I wouldn't sleep if I went home anyway," her mother assured him, placing a hand on her husband's arm and looking at him adoringly.

Tanner seemed unnaturally focused on her parents, as if he was watching every detail of their interaction. Did their obvious affection make him feel nervous?

"Then Whitney and I will see you first thing in the morning," Tanner said.

He really was great. Tanner didn't have to go with her. She kissed both of her parents. "Call if you need anything."

As she and Tanner drove through the early evening toward her grandparents' house Whitney reached over and rested her hand on his thigh. "Thank you for saving my father's life today."

"I don't know that I did that but you're welcome. I was pretty impressed by the cool head you kept. I've had nurses who showed less control in an emergency. If you ever want to give up matchmaking, I recommend you consider nursing or med school."

Whitney chuckled. "I think you're giving me too much credit but it's nice to hear praise."

Tanner pulled her parents' car into her grandparents' drive. He turned to look at her. "You should hear praise all the time. You're wonderful."

"You're pretty wonderful yourself." Her hand cupped his cheek and she gave him a kiss that held all the love she felt.

When they broke apart he wore a strange expression. Had Tanner sensed what she was offering him? They continued to look at each other. Had something subtly changed between them? Did she dare to hope he felt the love she did?

Tanner broke the spell of the moment with, "I guess we'd better go in and give your grandparents a report."

An hour later, she was driving her parents' car back to their house while Tanner followed her. She pulled it in the garage. Whitney had promised to pack her mother some clothes and her father a pair of pajamas and a few personal items. Tanner came inside to wait while she gathered things.

"So how long have your parents been married?" he asked from the living room.

"Thirty-one—no, thirty-two years." She stuck her head out of her parents' bedroom. "Why?"

"They just seem so happy together."

"They are," Whitney said from inside the bedroom.

"My parents fought all the time. I don't remember them being able to stay in the same room together over half an hour. They certainly couldn't stay in a hospital room together. Your parents must really love each other."

Whitney's heart filled with optimism. Tanner did recognize love. She stepped out of the room. "Yeah, they do."

Tanner was standing in front of a picture of her entire family. "No wonder you didn't understand why I didn't list that as necessary in my match."

"It was hard for me to understand at the time.

Now that you have told me about your parents I sort of understand. But that doesn't mean that you can't have love in your life." She looked directly at him. "I want what my parents have."

It took a moment before he said, "I can't promise that. I'm not even sure I know how to love like that."

Whitney stepped closer. "Maybe I can help you learn."

That night they walked hand and hand up the stairs to what was now their bedroom. When Whitney started to undress Tanner pushed her hands away. "Let me." He slowly removed her clothes, kissing each piece of flesh he exposed. With all her clothes on the floor, he quickly removed his. Tanner took her hand and led her to the bed.

"You are so amazing." He gently caressed her lips.

Whitney cupped his face with both her hands and kissed him with all the love she felt.

Tanner lifted her to the bed and joined her without breaking the contact. When they broke apart, he lay on his side and looked down at her. As his eyes raked her body, Whitney trembled. Tanner's look found hers, held.

"I don't know what you're doing to me, but I like who I am around you."

Whitney smiled. She knew what it was. Love.

Tanner kissed her again. When it went deeper Whitney nudged him to his back. She brought her lips to his chest over his heart. He inhaled sharply. Whitney captured his hands and held them at his sides. She kissed the curve of his neck and slowly slid over him. He moaned his pleasure. She continued to work her way up him, enjoying her skin touching his. She placed a kiss on his ear, eyebrow and finally his lips. She released his hands. He brought them to her hips, caressing her. He gently lifted her then slowly lowered her, joining them.

Their movements were deliberate and calm, yet there was an intensity between them they'd not had before. There was nothing of the frenzied coupling Tanner normally preferred. This time it was as if he was marking her as his.

Afterward, they lay in each other's arms for a long time without either of them speaking. Hope blossomed in Whitney.

The next few weeks passed much as the others had. For Tanner life was better than it had ever been yet there was something off he couldn't name.

After their lovemaking the night Whitney's father had gone into the hospital something had changed between them. The smiles Whitney gave him had an extra brightness to them. She touched him for no reason when she was walking by. She was waiting when he came home no matter what the time. The pleasure he found in bed was pure bliss and went beyond anything he'd ever experienced. Yet something nagged at him. As if he was missing something.

Whitney's father was home and doing well. He'd only visited with him once since he'd been released but Whitney gave Tanner a report each evening of his progress. When was the last time he had spoken to his father? Five years? Even his mother he only talked to a couple of times a year. The closeness, real caring, he saw in Whitney's family was a foreign concept for him.

All the attributes he appreciated most in Whitney he could see in some form in her parents. It made him uneasy on a level he didn't understand. Would Whitney continue to be happy with him? Would she demand more? Start treating him as his mother had his father?

Mr. Wilcox had been discharged the day after Mr. Thomason had been admitted. Mr. Wilcox's new heart was doing well. A friend had come to pick him up and had promised to see that he made it to his appointments.

"That young lady of ours came by to see me earlier this morning." Mr. Wilcox climbed into the wheelchair the orderly held for him.

Of course Whitney had.

Even with her father sick she wouldn't forget about someone else.

"She's a keeper. She has a big heart. To be loved by someone like that is a special thing. I know. I had it and miss it every day."

"Whitney is special." Tanner meant that. The more he was with her the more he found another facet of her personality he liked. It disturbed him that his emotional attachment was growing. He didn't want to think about that. Emotional attachment was something that he'd never wanted or planned to have.

They had been together almost two months when Tanner said at dinner one night, "We've been invited to a cocktail party on Friday evening at Malcolm and Marie's."

"We have?" Whitney sounded unsure.

"Will you go?"

"Do you really need me to?"

Hadn't she gotten past her fear of social situations after their weekend in Napa? "There'll be questions if you don't."

"Those events are just not my thing."

"But you were great in Napa. You don't give yourself enough credit. What's the problem?"

She left the table and walked to the kitchen sink, then confronted him. "The problem is that for over half my life I was made fun of or looked down on for my weight. I wasn't invited to or included in parties. Now I just plain don't care to be around those kinds of people. Up until a few years ago no one in that group would have given me the time of day."

"Why, Whitney Thomason, I had no idea you were such a snob."

"I am not! What I don't do is put myself in situations where I know I'll be made to feel inadequate."

Tanner turned in his chair to face her. "Did Malcolm and Marie make you feel that way in Napa?"

"Well, no." She crossed her arms over her chest.

"Do I make you feel that way?"

She backed up to the counter. "No-o-o... But not all the people are like you and the Jarvises."

"So you're going to let others control what you do in life?" Whitney winced. Tanner could tell that shot had hit its mark.

"No, but I don't have to be around them."

"I'll be there with you. Don't you trust me to support you?"

She came toward him. "I do, but I just think you'd be better off at those events without some insecure woman to worry about."

He faced her. "Has it occurred to you that I might need your support at the party? That social situations might not be my 'thing' either?"

"Why would you need my support? You're a successful heart surgeon, you're gorgeous and intelligent—who wouldn't enjoy your company?"

"Apparently you." Tanner sounded hurt, which he was. "I'm still trying to get that promotion. Making small talk is a little nerve-racking for me as well."

Whitney studied him for a minute. "I had no idea you felt that way. You seem to have so much confidence wherever you go."

"Now you know another one of my secrets."

She came back to the table and just before she sat he grabbed her and pulled her onto his lap. "So will you go with me?"

"I guess we're in it together."

Tanner kissed her. "About that gorgeous and intelligent remark, you really think so?"

She slapped his shoulder. "Now you're just fishing for compliments."

He chuckled. "That's because I like hearing you say them. They sound extra good coming out of your pretty mouth."

"Maybe for another kiss I could say more."

"For a kiss you don't have to say anything." His mouth found hers.

Whitney didn't make a habit of buying new clothes often but she had found that her wardrobe had almost completely changed since she and Tanner had started seeing each other. He liked to see her in clothes that fit her form and she'd taken to wearing less baggy clothes. Even her nightclothes, if she wore any, were flimsy gowns with lace and bows that had little substance. Tanner had slowly seen to it that all her granny gowns went out with the trash. She didn't mind. In fact, she rather liked the person she was becoming with Tanner.

On her own initiative, she went shopping for a dress for the cocktail party. She found a simply cut black A-line that she felt confident wearing. At home that evening, Tanner only added to her self-assurance when he saw her enter the living room where he was waiting.

He stood and came toward her. Taking her hand, he turned her around and whistled. "If I didn't need to show up for this party I'd say forget it and spend the rest of the night taking that dress off you."

"You do have a way of making a girl feel good." She kissed him. "You look superb yourself."

He did, dressed in his dark suit with a light blue tie. The man was almost too handsome to look at. It gave her a boost of confidence just being seen with him. But what she liked most about him couldn't be seen. Tanner was such a fine person.

An hour later they arrived at the Jarvises'.

They were greeted warmly and Whitney was truly glad to see them both. She and Tanner had agreed on the way over that as soon as possible they would own up to their deception in Napa.

"Malcolm, Marie, Whitney and I owe you both an apology. Really me more than Whitney. I convinced her to pretend that she was my girlfriend in Napa when she was actually working as my matchmaker."

"But you're both here together now so it must have worked." Marie smiled broadly.

Tanner put his arm around Whitney's waist and brought her close. "Yes, it did."

"Then no harm was done." Malcolm patted him on the back.

"Did I hear someone say something about a matchmaker?"

Whitney cringed at the sound of Charlotte's voice. Squaring her shoulders, she turned and faced the woman. "I'm a matchmaker."

"Who needs a matchmaker?" Charlotte's voice held disgust.

Malcolm said, "Apparently Marie and I did. We met though a matchmaking service."

The look on Charlotte's face was almost comical. "If you'll excuse me, I think Max is looking for me."

Charlotte left to the sound of two couples'

laughter. Whitney couldn't help feeling both vindicated and sorry for her.

Tanner remained close throughout the rest of the evening and Whitney found she was enjoying herself. She liked the new person she was becoming. The one who felt good about her life.

She had excused herself and was in the hallway on the way to the restroom when she overheard some women talking in an alcove.

"I can't believe that woman Mark is with. She has an unbelievable body."

"Yeah. He went out and got him a thin one," another woman said.

"He divorced Mildred after she became so large," the first woman said. "I heard he said he needed someone who could help his career, not someone he wanted to hide."

Heat flooded Whitney. At one time that could have been her they were talking about.

A third voice said, "You're just saying that because he won't give you a second look."

Whitney shuddered. These were part of Tanner's social circle. Were these the type of people she would be forced into being around for the rest of her life?

"And that woman Tanner is with." Her tone held a note of disgust. "I know her name from somewhere. I just can't figure out where."

"Charlotte said she's a matchmaker. Can you imagine?"

"I know where I've seen her before. She went to college with me. She was President of the Literary Society. I knew I recognized her name. She used to be huge."

"A fat matchmaker," one of them cackled.

Whitney had heard that kind of talk before. She didn't like it any better now.

"She's not fat now."

"No, she isn't, but I wonder how she managed to snag that gorgeous Tanner. I wonder if he knows she was once so heavy."

Whitney had heard enough. She felt sick. Moisture filled her eyes. She wanted to get out of there. Turning, she headed down the hall again in search of Tanner.

As she reached him, he took one look at her and demanded, "What's wrong?"

"I'd like to go now." She worked not to have a quiver in her voice.

Tanner touched her arm. "Are you not feeling well?"

She pulled away. "You could say that."

A perplexed look came over his face. "Let's say our goodbyes to Malcolm and Marie then we can go."

"Why don't you do that for me? I'll wait for you in the car."

Tanner looked at her closely. "What's going on? You feeling ill?"

"I'll tell you when we get home." Whitney made her way toward the front door.

She had already called for the car by the time Tanner joined her. The valet pulled up in front of them before Tanner could start asking questions.

He helped her in then went around and slid into the driver's seat. They were out on the road when he asked, "Do you want to tell me what happened back there?"

CHAPTER NINE

TANNER'S TONE REMINDED Whitney too much of how he had sounded when he'd demanded that she go with him to Napa. He wasn't going to leave her any choice but to answer. "Can we please just talk about it when we get home?"

He glanced at her. "Okay, but I'll accept nothing short of a full explanation."

For the next three-quarters of an hour they said nothing. Tanner glanced at her a couple of times with concern. Which only made what she was going to have to say worse. Whitney searched for a way out of what she knew was coming. She was going to give up everything she had ever dreamed of or hoped for. A burning sensation rolled in her middle. Whitney crossed her arms over her stomach. She might truly be sick.

What could she do to stop herself from destroying her life? How could she not? She couldn't live thinking she was inadequate every time she and Tanner went out. That Tanner might one day be disappointed in her. Leave her. Those old insecurities she'd thought she'd put away when she had lost weight hadn't been far below the surface.

Anyway, Tanner had made it clear weeks ago when they had met to start looking for a mate for him that he was only interested in a mutually beneficial relationship. Not love. She wanted love or nothing. There had not been one word about loving her in the weeks they had been together. There might never be. How was she supposed to gain his love if she couldn't even handle herself at one of his social gatherings without falling apart?

They weren't going to work. It was best to call it quits now before either one of them got in any deeper. Only it was too late for her. She loved him beyond measure.

At her house Tanner helped her out of the car. He followed her into the living room. She went to stand near the fireplace behind a chair. She needed it to provide her support.

Tanner stood in the middle of the room, waiting.

That nauseated feeling intensified. Only with a determination she would have sworn she didn't possess did Whitney meet his look. What she had to say must be said.

"Whitney, what happened?" There was alarm in his voice. "Are you okay?"

She sadly shook her head. "Tanner, we're not going to work."

"What?" He started toward her.

She put out a hand to stop him. "Us as a couple isn't going to work."

He came to an abrupt halt. "I thought we were working just fine until an hour ago. Now I'm just confused. Could you tell me what the problem is?"

What she wouldn't give to have him quit glaring at her. Hurt had seeped into his eyes. She said as clearly as she could, "I overheard some women talking about one of the ladies being fat. They even had something to say about me being with you. I can't tolerate that backbiting. I know that social events are important to your career but I can't do it. I spent too much of my life being treated as a second-class citizen. I won't go there again."

His look turned incredulous. "You've got to be kidding! All of this is about a few women being bitchy?"

She gripped the chair. How could she make him understand? A lifetime of people thinking you're less of a person because your body hung over a chair, your plate was piled full, your clothes baggy. Being judged and found wanting. Those emotions weren't easily pushed aside.

"It's more than that. I'm not who you need. I'll

end up disappointing you. What if I gain weight? I can so easily. I have to watch it all the time."

He put out his hands as if pleading. "Hell, you're old enough and smart enough to know that people are the same everywhere. They're going to talk. What they say doesn't matter."

"I wish that was true. But it's hard for me to push away those old feelings of not being good enough. Your friends and associates are the type who used to put me down or, worse, not include me. I don't want to embarrass you. Be an embarrassment to you."

Tanner's hands had fallen to his sides and he all but shouted, "That's not going to happen."

"You don't know that." Whitney worked to keep her voice even and calm while her heart raced in her chest. "We're deluding ourselves. You hired me to find you the 'right match.' I'm not it."

"There has to be more to this than women talking. You couldn't possibly be that insecure. Or think so little of me. I've never said anything but positive things about your looks. I think you are beautiful." His disbelief circled around them like an angry animal.

"That's because you've never known what it's like, being an outsider," she said, unable to meet his blazing eyes.

"The hell I haven't." He stepped toward her.

"What do you think it was like to live with my parents? I never knew if my father was coming home or how crazy my mother would be when he did. My brother and I never had any idea what to expect. At least you had functional parents. A place to live where all the focus wasn't on what your parents wanted. You felt loved."

She gripped the chair, glad for its support. Maybe he did understand what it was like to have apprehensions but she wasn't going to keep putting herself into the kind of situation she'd been in tonight. "I don't know what you want from me."

"I was going to ask you to marry me."

Her look zeroed in on his. "What? As a business merger or a declaration of love?"

Tanner didn't come any closer. "You knew from our first meeting that love wasn't part of the deal."

And she had. But she had hoped he would change his mind. Would slowly come to know love through her actions toward him. "That's what you said."

He dipped his chin and cocked a brow. "You didn't believe me?"

"Yes, but I thought you'd change when you found the right woman."

His chuckle had no real humor to it. "Whitney, I know I've made it perfectly clear what I am looking for in a wife. I'm sure I've not misled you even once."

"That's just it. I want something you can't or won't give." She moved to stand beside the chair. "I love you and I want you to love me in return. You refuse. I won't settle for less. I've seen what a loving relationship can be with my grandparents and parents. I deserve the same.

"You do as well but you're so sure that it doesn't exist or that you'll be so dependent on another person for happiness that you push that happiness away. I've shown you love in every way I know how in the last few months. Mind, body and soul. Yet you won't accept it. I need someone in my life who wants me for more than laughs and companionship or good sex."

"I'll have you know that sex between us is better than good. And I want you to have my children. You would be a wonderful mother."

Whitney slowly shook her head, sadness overtaking her. "You just don't get it. The sex is so great because I'm making love to you. But I still won't bring a child into a loveless marriage. You're so fearful that you're going to end up acting like your mother that you can't let anyone in. The thing is that you act more like your father. Taking the love and life you could have and throwing it back in my face."

Tanner looked as if she'd socked him on the chin, dazed him. She had hit a nerve. A very exposed one. Whitney stepped back a pace. "I'm sorry. I shouldn't have said that."

As if performing a magic trick, Tanner made a transformation. Straightening his shoulders and with all the fire leaving his eyes, he smiled tightly at her. He shoved his hands in his pockets. His demeanor became as cold as the night air coming off the San Francisco Bay in winter. "You may be right about that. But this just proves that love isn't worth the hurt.

"Since we're being so open here, let me tell you a few things. Not everyone wants a pie-in-the-sky, everything-is-rosy marriage. Some people just want peace in their life. A haven to come home to where people coexist, have common interests and mutual respect. Maybe some people, you included, think that a loving marriage is the goal in life. Me, I don't know how to do that. And I've never said or implied that I did.

"Another thing. You can't punish me for what people did to you in your past. You can't live worried about what people might do and say now. You're not the person you were when you were heavy. It's rather vain for you to think everyone is judging you. People like your ex-fiancé disappoint others. I'm not your ex. I don't have to love you to be supportive and stand beside you. I think I have proved that more than once."

Whitney shrank back. He had proved his loyalty. Still, she wanted his heart.

"One more thing." He raised a finger in the air. "Not once have I ever said I give a damn about your weight. Even when I gave you a list of what I was looking for in a mate, I didn't once say anything about the woman being thin. All of that is in—" he pointed his finger at her "—your head.

"Don't bother asking me to leave. I'm gone. Throw my stuff in a bag. Put it on the front stoop. Text me and I'll come and get it. That way I won't ever bother you again."

Seconds later her front door closed with a shudder of the stained glass that coincided with her howl of agony.

It had been three weeks since Tanner had left Whitney's and he still didn't feel any better. He'd never been so blindsided in his life. Whitney's announcement that their relationship wasn't working had been news to him. She'd completely overreacted to what amounted to gossip. Those women didn't matter. People talked all the time. What mattered was what was best for Whitney and him. They enjoyed the same things, were great together in bed. Wanted the same things out of life. Maybe that wasn't exactly right. She wanted love, needed it from him. Did he even understand the emotion? Was he capable of giving it if he did?

He wanted to put his hand through a wall or shake Whitney until he shook some sense into her.

When he'd left her place he'd driven to his apartment, which he'd been thinking of selling because things between him and Whitney had been going so well. That was over. Entering the cold, sterile-looking place after staying in Whitney's warm and inviting home made him more depressed. She'd added vitality to his life.

More times than he could count he'd been hurt by his parents' actions but he had never felt this gnawing, snarling anger and frustration eating away at him that he had now. It affected every part of his life. Including his work. His staff was starting to give him looks and make hushed comments under their breath after he had given an order. He was trying to get a promotion and his staff was tiptoeing around him.

The nights were the worst. Especially when he did doze off and woke reaching for her on the other side of the bed. Most of the time he just paced the floor or stayed at the hospital. Eyedrops had become a staple because he never seemed to close his eyes. If he did, Whitney's smiling face invaded his mind. Her swishing her butt as she sang to a song while cooking dinner. Whitney's look of bliss as she found her release.

He slammed his hand down on his desk, making the pen beside it jump. This had to stop.

Punching the button on the desk phone, he ran back through the messages until he found hers, leaving him the name of the other matchmaker. It was time to move on.

The sound of Whitney's clear voice almost dissolved his resolve. He missed her with every fiber of his being. Even his clothes smelled of her.

He'd gone by her place. A bag had sat on the stoop, just as he'd requested. When he'd got it home and opened it, the smell of her had wafted around him. He'd felt sucker punched. Inside the bag had been his clothes, neatly folded and arranged with care. She'd still been taking care of him. The smell had lingered to the point where he'd stuffed all the clothing back into the bag and taken them to the cleaners.

Tanner picked up the pen and quickly jotted the number down that Whitney had left in the message. He didn't want to have to listen twice. With a punch of his finger he deleted the communication. That ended any temptation to hear it again.

He was tied in knots and it was time to get undone. The first step was to call this new matchmaker and start the process of finding someone who fit his requirements. Someone who didn't see love as the main ingredient. He would make the call as soon as he saw his afternoon clinic patients. The first on the list was Mr. Wilcox. Whitney had even managed to take some of the pleasure out of seeing the older man. Why had he let her permeate his working life? He was paying for it dearly. And was afraid he'd be doing so for a long time to come.

Tanner opened the door to the small but functional examination room. Mr. Wilcox sat on the exam table with his shirt off. "Hello. How're you feeling?" Tanner asked.

"I'm fine except for the fact that I'm freezing to death. You ask us to strip down then leave us in a cold room."

That was one of many things he liked about Mr. Wilcox. The man said what he thought. Not unlike Whitney. "Sorry about that. Let me give you a listen then you can get dressed."

Tanner pulled his stethoscope from around his neck. Mr. Wilcox was doing well. His heart was working as expected and so far there was no major rejection. Tanner fully believed he would live many more years. Minutes later he said, "You sound good. You can put your shirt on now." He gave Mr. Wilcox a steady hand to hold as he climbed down from the table.

Mr. Wilcox slid an arm into a sleeve of his shirt and said, "So how's your lady doing?"

The one subject Tanner didn't what to talk about. His lady. Whitney had been. He'd been happy then.

"She's fine."

Mr. Wilcox looked up from buttoning his shirt. "That doesn't sound so fine."

Tanner acted as if he was writing on the chart. "It's not. We broke up."

"I'm sorry to hear that. But you know the old saying, 'If it's worth having it's worth fighting for.' I would say that one is worth fighting for."

"I don't think it matters. We want two different things out of life."

Mr. Wilcox nodded with his lips pursed as if in thought. "That so? I think I'd be changing what I want to keep her."

Could he do that? Tell her that he loved her? Did he?

"It's good to see you, Mr. Wilcox. Call if you need us, otherwise I'll see you in two months."

"Sounds good. Hey, you know love isn't always easy but it's always worth it."

There was that word again. Love. That wasn't the kind of relationship he wanted. Yet there was an ache where his heart was that was saying differently.

His fourth patient for the afternoon was a middle-aged woman who had progressively gotten sicker and sicker. He would soon have to place her on the transplant list.

Tanner plastered on a congenial smile and entered the room. "Hello, Mrs. Culpepper."

"Hi, Dr. Locke. I'd like you to meet my husband, Henry."

The man with graying hair at his temples stood. He and Tanner shook hands.

"Do you mind if I give you a listen, Mrs. Culpepper?" Tanner said as he removed his stethoscope.

"That's what I'm here for." She smiled and sat straighter on the exam table.

Tanner listened carefully to the slow and sluggish organ in her chest. Even her breathing was taking on a more labored sound. "Give me a sec. I need to have a look at your X-rays." Tanner typed his security code into the computer and pulled up Mrs. Culpepper's chart. With another click the picture she had just taken in the X-ray department came up on the screen. There it was, the oversize heart of the thin woman sitting before him.

He looked at Mrs. Culpepper. "I'm going to let you get dressed and have you meet me down the hall in the conference room where we can talk more comfortably. Lisa, my nurse, will be in to show you the way."

A distressed look came over her face but she nodded and slid off the table to stand. Her husband hurried to help her.

A few minutes later Tanner entered a room furnished with a serviceable table and six chairs. His nurse assistant, Lisa, and the Culpeppers were already waiting for him. Tanner took a chair facing them. Mrs. Culpepper looked close to tears. She must fear what was coming. This was the least enjoyable part of Tanner's job. Mr. Culpepper placed a hand on hers resting on the table. He too must sense what Tanner was planning to say.

"It's time, isn't it?" Mrs. Culpepper said.

Tanner nodded. "It is."

Her husband gently squeezed her hand. "We'll get through this together. That's what we do."

She looked at him. The bond between them was obvious. "I know I can count on you."

Why had Tanner never noticed that in couples before? Since Whitney had come into his life he seemed to see loving couples everywhere where he'd seen none before. For the first time in his life he'd begun to want that. But he'd thrown it back in Whitney's face when she'd offered it.

"We'll start the process of getting you listed on the United Network for Organ Sharing today. There'll be further tests in the days ahead. Lisa will help you with those."

The couple's eyes glistened with moisture as they clung together.

Could the day get any worse? He'd bet everything he owned that Whitney would show that same loving concern if her husband was ill. Because she would love him. Their souls would be united. Would a wife based on his list care about him in the same way?

"So what do we need to do?" Mr. Culpepper asked.

The man saw his wife's health as a partnership. Why hadn't Tanner noticed that in his patients before? The Culpeppers couldn't be the only ones who felt that way. Had he just been choosing to ignore how people who loved each other acted? Was he so scared of loving or being loved that he was running from it? Wasn't that what Whitney had accused him of?

Could he live with someone who loved him without becoming emotionally invested himself? Not if he wanted Whitney. She would demand it of him. Could he give it? What he needed to understand was why his father had refused to accept it.

Half an hour later he left the Culpeppers with Lisa and returned to his office. He found the piece of paper he'd written the matchmaker's name on and crumbled it into a ball then tossed it into the trash. He already knew who his match was. Now all he had to do was be worthy of her. Find some way of meeting her halfway. That could only come from understanding why his parents had had such a dysfunctional relationship.

He picked up his phone. When a man answered Tanner said, "Dad. It's Tanner. Can I come down to see you this weekend?"

Tanner had driven faster than the speed limit, so he'd made good time on his way south on the coast road to Santa Barbara. He'd not seen his father in over five years and even then it had been brief and tense. There was no common ground for a relationship between them. That wouldn't change but Tanner needed to try to get some answers, a little understanding. There was no doubt he would be digging up painful memories but if he wanted to have the life he was dreaming of, finding that peace, he had to try to come to grips with his childhood.

Whitney had said he was like his father. The more he thought about it the more he tended to agree. So why was he like the man he disliked so much? Because he'd been so afraid of being hurt, like his mother had been?

His father had been surprised to hear from him. Rightfully so. There was a long pause when Tanner had asked if he could visit.

"Why?" had been his father's response.

"I have some questions I need answered."

Again there was a long pause. "Come on. I can't promise you'll like what you hear."

At least his father was willing to listen to the questions.

Tanner turned into his father's drive just before lunchtime. He had a simple one-story home that was well kept in a subdivision about five miles from the beach.

He and his father had agreed to go out to eat. Tanner felt they needed a neutral zone for the possibly tense discussion they were to have. His father had remarried while Tanner had been in med school but he had never met his new wife. Tanner had hardly stepped out of the car before his father exited the house and walked toward him. He was an older version of what Tanner saw in the mirror. He was like his father in more ways than one.

"Hello, Tanner."

"Hi, Dad. It's nice to see you." To his amazement Tanner actually meant it.

"Good to see you as well. The restaurant is just half a mile from here."

Was he protecting his wife from what might be said between them by not inviting Tanner in? "Okay. Would you like to ride with me?"

For a second Tanner thought his father might say no. "That'll work."

His father had picked a local place with plenty of room between the tables. Tanner was glad. They wouldn't easily be overheard. It wasn't until they were settled at their table, drinks served and orders taken, that Tanner said, "I have some questions about you and Mom."

Seeing his father's expression, Tanner was glad he'd requested a quiet spot off to the side. This discussion might be more difficult than he'd expected.

"Just what do you want to know?" His father fiddled with his napkin.

"Why you even married? Why were you never around? Did you even love her? Us?"

His father sighed deeply. "I should have had this discussion with you and Mark a long time ago but it was easier not to. I ought to have known it would happen one day. Yes, I loved your mother. Married her because I did. I've always loved you and Mark."

"So why did you and Mother always act like you were so unhappy?"

"Because we were. Your mother was so jealous. She smothered me. It wasn't that way so much at first. But as time went on she became obsessed. She'd accuse me of seeing other women. I wasn't but there was no convincing her. I tried to keep it all from you and your brother. We went to counseling but nothing worked. So when I had a chance to take a job traveling, I did, hoping that things would be better if I wasn't around so much. But that only made the situation worse when I came home. Her jealousy killed my love and then our marriage. I would have taken you and Mark with me but you were all she had. I feared she might take her life if I did that."

"You know that I hated you for how you treated her." Tanner couldn't keep his bitterness out of his voice. He'd lived with it too long.

"I know. But I thought it better for you to hate me than her."

His father had loved him enough to make that sacrifice. Was that the type of love Whitney had been showing him? She understood sacrificial love over possessive love. He'd still been the kid that couldn't see the difference.

"Dad, why have you never said anything? Mark and I have been adults for a long time."

He shrugged. "It wouldn't have changed anything."

"Yeah, it would have. I've had a wonderful

woman in my life who I wasn't willing to love because I didn't think it was possible to have a marriage based on emotion."

There was a sheen of moisture in his father's eyes. "Tanner, I never meant for you to feel that way. I'm sorry. Will you tell me about her?"

Over the next few minutes Tanner shared how he and Whitney had met. Why they had broken up.

"Life is too short to spend it without love," his father said.

"Another man told me the same thing recently."

His father met his look. "So what're you going to do?"

"Beg her to forgive me for being an idiot and shout from the Golden Gate Bridge that I love her."

His father's smile was genuine for the first time. "That sounds like a good start. Then tell her that every day for the rest of your life."

"I will."

During the meal they caught up on what they had missed in each other's lives. When they returned to his father's house he invited Tanner in to meet his wife. Tanner hesitated but then agreed.

"Julie, I'm home," his father called as they came in the front door.

The living room looked comfortable. Lived in, much like Whitney's. A place that made you feel welcome.

His father kissed the petite brown-haired woman on the cheek and put his arm around her waist when she joined them. That was something Tanner had never seen him do with his mother.

"Tanner, I'd like you to meet my wife, Julie. Julie, this is Tanner."

Julie surprised him by hugging him. Her smile was warm and inviting. "It's so nice to meet you. Your father brags about you all the time."

Tanner looked at his father, who shrugged and smiled affectionately at Julie. "Honey, don't tell all my secrets."

"Well, it's true. Why don't we sit down and I can find out if your father has been telling me the truth?"

Tanner couldn't help but smile. The warmth Julie exuded made him feel at ease. He liked her. She sat close to his father on the sofa and every so often she touched him when she was making a point. Julie obviously cared for his father. There was a happiness about him Tanner had never seen before. To his amazement Tanner was glad for him.

As Tanner was leaving his father called out, "Let me know how it goes with Whitney."

"I will." The relationship between his father

and himself wasn't what it should be but they had made a step forward.

Now Tanner had to face Whitney. Could he possibly let go enough to admit how he felt about her? If he wanted Whitney, he'd have to. What sickened him was that he hadn't recognized her love when she'd given it. He'd had it right there in front of him and he hadn't grabbed it. After all, he did love her. Had for a long time.

Whitney had cried to the point of being sick. In the past there had been days when people had hurt her feelings and she'd been upset but nothing matched the agony she felt over the loss of Tanner. His absence was a void she couldn't fill.

She had managed to place Tanner's clothes in a bag and text him but it had almost torn her heart out. Against her better judgment she'd kept one of his T-shirts. It was an unhealthy thing to do but she'd become so accustomed to having him next to her in bed that she put the shirt under the spare pillow and pulled it out to smell it before she went to sleep. When she could sleep.

So much time had passed since she had spoken to her parents they'd become concerned enough to check on her. When they did she gave them a blurry-eyed, tearful and painfully short version of what had happened. They were supportive and worried but in the end there wasn't anything they could do to help. As they were leaving her mother said, "We never know what life will give us. Never give up."

Whitney knew life sent you experiences and people that you never expected. Tanner had proved that. The problem was this time she was the one who had told Tanner to go. It had been the right decision but it still hurt.

In the middle of the second week she'd been in mourning for Tanner a new client called. That was the catalyst that started bringing her out of the darkness. She needed to keep herself busy for sanity's sake. To do that she was going to have to start clawing her way back to being a functioning adult again. She took a bath and washed her hair before sitting down at the computer. To her horror Tanner's profile was the first one to appear in her business file.

She looked at his smiling face for too long before she deleted it. She wouldn't need his profile any longer. Was he already dating other matches? The idea was crushing. But she had pushed him away. He was free to do as he pleased.

She kept repeating like a mantra that she had done it for their own good. Love was important to her. Necessary and nonnegotiable. For Tanner it was unimportant. He had issues that he needed to resolve. He'd stated clearly that he believed she did as well.

Hadn't she dealt with those long ago?

Whitney looked around the kitchen where bags of chips and dessert snack covers cluttered the table and counter. She'd turned to food again to sooth her stress and fear. Jumping up, she gathered the litter and uneaten junk food, cramming it in the garbage can. That too had to stop. Returning to her desk, she picked up her phone and punched in the number to speed dial the overeating support group she'd once attended. It was time to get her life back on track without Tanner.

Over the next two days she set up two socials and made an appointment to meet a new client. She didn't feel alive yet but at least she was making an effort.

Her client was a woman of about her own age. In fact, she looked familiar. Extremely attractive, she still seemed a little unsure of herself. She kept looking around as if she were expecting someone to catch her doing something she shouldn't. Her name was familiar too. Lauren Phillips.

High school. That was it! She'd been one of the popular girls. The one who'd got all the boys. Now she needed Whitney to help her make a match.

"I believe we went to high school together," Whitney said at their meeting.

Lauren studied her but there was no recognition in her eyes. "I'm sorry, I don't remember you. High school was a tough time for me. My parents were getting a divorce. I didn't pay much attention to anyone but myself."

"It's okay. We can't remember everyone." Whitney meant it. Before Tanner she would have been resentful of Lauren but now she understood too clearly that no matter how someone might act on the outside, they could still have problems. "So how can I help you?"

"I am looking for companionship. Someone who enjoys the same things I do," Lauren answered. "I want someone who's looking to get serious and settle down. All the guys I meet are just interested in my looks. I want someone who sees past that."

Whitney had had that with Tanner. What if she had waited longer? Maybe Tanner would have come around to loving her. He had certainly accepted her for who she was. Instead of giving him any real chance, she'd let her insecurities control her. How was she supposed to match other people when she couldn't handle her own? Her self-doubt had left her with nothing.

How he must hate her.

Whitney pushed through the glass door of the community center for the first time in years. It would be tough to join the Happier You support group again but these were her people and here she would be accepted without question. It had taken her years to admit she needed support when she'd lost weight. She'd started managing her eating again but what she had really been looking for had been the emotional care. The help for what had been behind her overeating. The Happier You group had given her that.

She walked down the hall to the classroom. Inside she found the circle of chairs she expected and a few people already in them. She smiled in their direction and took a seat. Another couple of people entered before Margaret, the facilitator, showed up.

"Whitney Thomason, is that you?"

"It is." Whitney stood and hugged the woman.

"So what brings you here tonight?"

"I guess just for a reminder of how far I've come," Whitney said.

"So it's like that?"

Whitney nodded.

An hour and a half later Whitney was feeling strong enough to face the world and Tanner as well. While others had been talking she had been formulating a plan. She would write Tanner a letter. Tell him that she was sorry for treating him the way she had.

She was on her way out of the room when Margaret called after her. Whitney turned.

"Hold on a minute. I want to ask you something."

Whitney waited until Margaret finished speaking to the last person and came to her. "What's up?"

"I was wondering if you would consider something," Margaret said.

"What's that?"

Margaret moved a chair back into place. "Taking over this group for me. I have a chance to start one over near my house but can't leave this one high and dry. I think you would be great at it."

Her lead a group? "Can I think about it? Get back to you?"

"Sure. Just don't take too long."

Whitney didn't know if she could. She had always been in the background. "I'll let you know something by next week."

"Perfect."

Whitney made it to the door before Margaret said, "You know, you've changed, Whitney. There is more confidence about you. And you look great. Whatever is causing it, keep doing it."

That was because of Tanner. He'd made her feel supported, confident. Even though she'd pushed him away, he had left her that gift.

"Thanks, Margaret."

At home that evening Whitney pulled out a piece of stationery. She was going to write that letter. After careful thought she decided that a text or email message was too impersonal. She had to show that she meant what she wrote, was making a true effort.

Dear Tanner...

She marked that out.

Tanner,
   I want you to know that I'm sorry for the way I treated you. You did not deserve it. I should not have assumed the worst of you, your friends or colleagues. I should have accepted your support for what it was, just that.
   Please know that in many ways you've helped me grow as a person, and for that I will always be grateful.
   I wish you well always.
   Whitney

She rubbed the moisture under her eyes as she reread the note. To the point with no emotion. Folding it perfectly, she slipped it into an envelope and addressed it to his hospital office. Not allowing herself to rethink it, she put it in the mailbox beside the front door for pickup the next day.

Now it was time to move on. The door with Tanner's name on it was closed.

CHAPTER TEN

TANNER ONLY HAD a few minutes before he was due in surgery to read the mail his secretary had left in a stack on his desk. He picked up a letter that looked out of place. His chest tightened. Whitney's handwriting. Why would she be writing to him? Tearing it open, he scanned the brief but sincere note.

His heart filled with hope. Maybe there was a chance with her after all. She was at least opening a door for him to approach. Now if he just knocked loud enough she'd have no choice but to let him in. He was going to start working on making that happen right away.

Tanner picked up the phone. When the man on the other end answered Tanner said, "Hey, Charlie, I need a favor."

"What's that?"

Tanner wasted no time in saying, "I need you to hire a matchmaker."

"I don't think my wife would like that." Charlie chuckled.

"No, I need you to pretend you need a matchmaker. I'll go in your place." Tanner couldn't afford for this to go wrong.

"You're not making any sense. Why can't you just do it?"

Tanner explained he wasn't sure that Whitney would meet him if he didn't surprise her. That he needed to get her to a public place so she was more likely to hear him out. "You do this for me and I'll take your calls for a month."

"Wow, you want this pretty bad."

"I do."

"Then it's a deal. What's the number?"

A few days later Charlie called back with a date and time at Café Lombard. "Good luck, man. She must be pretty special to go to this kind of trouble."

"She is. Thanks."

Three days later Malcolm stopped him in the hallway outside the CICU. "Tanner, can I have a word with you?"

"I've only got a second." He was due to meet Whitney in two hours and he wouldn't be late. Tanner was anxious and hoped Malcolm wouldn't be long-winded.

Malcolm smiled. "I wanted to give you a

heads-up on this. The board met last night. You got the directorship."

Tanner should have been super excited but all he could think about was meeting Whitney. The directorship paled in comparison to winning Whitney back. He took a few steps backward, anxious to leave. "Thanks for letting me know."

Malcolm gave him a quizzical look. "Maybe you and Whitney would like to have dinner with us to celebrate."

"I'll let you know," Tanner called over his shoulder as he headed down the hall.

Two hours later Tanner sat at a table in the patio area of the café where he and Whitney had met his prospective matches. What would her reaction be when she saw him? Would she turn and walk away? Would she listen to him?

His pulse jumped. There she was. His heart swelled. She looked beautiful. He'd missed her so much that it had almost become a tangible thing he carried.

Wearing a sky blue dress that fit her torso then flared gently around her legs, Whitney looked nothing like the dowdy shopkeeper of old. There was a spring in her step that was new. A sick feeling came over him. What had put that there? Had she found someone new? Maybe she wasn't missing him as much as he was her.

Tanner saw the second her step faltered as she

crossed the street. She'd seen him. Their gazes met. He held his apprehension in check by sheer will. Standing, he never took his eyes off her. She continued toward him at a slower pace.

When she reached him he said, "Will you join me?"

"I have—" she cleared her throat "—to meet a client."

"I'm the client."

"What?" She looked as if she might run.

He quickly said, "I wasn't sure you'd meet me so I asked a friend to pretend to need a match."

She sighed and her shoulders slumped. "Tanner, I don't have time to waste with games."

"I'm not playing a game." It was his life they were talking about here. He pulled out a chair. "Please, join me for just a minute."

For a second he feared she was going to say no but she reluctantly sat, her hands clutching her purse. "What's this all about?"

"I was wondering if you could help me find someone to love and who will love me?"

Me. Me. Me. Whitney wanted to shout.

Did he mean it? Could she trust that she had heard him right? He had said love. Something he'd said he wouldn't give. Did she dare hope? She watched him closely. "What're you talking about? I thought we settled this weeks ago. I'm not the right matchmaker for you."

"You're usually not this slow to catch on," Tanner said with a smile.

"To what?" Now he was starting to irritate her.

"*You're* my perfect match. I'm telling you I *love* you. I hope you still feel the same about me."

Whitney's hands trembled. She could hardly breathe. She'd never thought she'd hear him say that. Could her dreams be coming true?

Tanner was looking at her with anticipation and a touch of uncertainty. Was he afraid she might turn him away? With his experience with love he might think it was something that came and went easily. Hers lasted forever.

She jumped to her feet and flung herself into his arms. His hands went to her waist, giving her a furious hug. Her arms circled his neck and her mouth found his. His kiss was all about acceptance and pleasure. But more than that—love.

As Tanner began deepening the kiss someone behind them said, "Excuse me."

They broke apart. Heat ran into Whitney's face. She looked at Tanner and he had a bashful look on his as well. They had both forgotten they were in a public place. Whitney eased back into her chair.

"Sorry," Tanner said to the young waitress. "She can't keep her hands off me."

"Tanner!"

He smiled and gave her an innocent look. "It's true. Would you like something?"

Whitney glanced at the waitress then said to Tanner, "What I'd really like to do is go home."

He asked, "I'm invited?"

Whitney smiled brightly. "You are. We need to talk."

"I agree." Tanner stood and dug in his pocket, pulling out a bill. After giving it to the surprised waitress, he offered a hand to Whitney.

Grinning and feeling like the sun was shining just for her, Whitney slipped her hand into Tanner's larger secure one. They made their way around a few tables and out to the sidewalk. Tanner led her down the street toward where his car was parked.

"Where's your car?"

"I took a streetcar and walked," she said.

They continued down the hill and Tanner said, "Thank you for your letter."

"It was the least I could do. I was pretty ugly to you." She'd spend the rest of her life making that up to him.

Opening the car door for her, Tanner said, "That you were."

She gave him a teasing swat on the arm. "But you deserved it."

"We'll discuss that more when we get to your

house." He pulled out of his parking space and headed up the street. When he had moved into the rhythm of the traffic he took her hand and placed it on his thigh under his. She'd come home. It felt so good to have his touch again. But they still had things to discuss.

It didn't take long until Tanner slid the car to a stop in front of her house. She climbed out as he did and met him on the sidewalk. "Would you rather walk awhile or go inside to talk?"

"I think we'd better walk." Tanner took her hand again. "If I get you behind a closed door my mind is going to be on other things besides talking."

Tanner's raspy voice sent a shiver down her spine. "Walk it is."

They started up the sidewalk along the grassy knoll across the street from her home.

"Whitney, I'm sorry I've been such an idiot. The truth is I've been in love with you since you came to my rescue in the balloon. I just didn't want to admit it. My parents and what I saw in their marriage screwed me up."

"No more than the insecurities I carry around with me because I was once fat."

"Yeah, but my issues weren't even based on facts. It turns out that my father loved my mother. She was just so jealous that she killed it."

Whitney stopped and looked at him. "How did you find that out?"

"I went to see my father the other weekend. We had lunch together. He didn't much want to answer my questions but he did. Turns out he's been protecting my mother all along."

"Really?"

"Yeah. He let my brother and me believe he was the bad guy so that we wouldn't blame my mother. He wanted us to love her." There was acceptance in his voice she'd not heard when he'd spoken of his parents before.

"It takes a special person to sacrifice themselves for another." She started up the sidewalk again.

"I hadn't thought about it like that. It figures a woman with a big heart herself would see it that way." Tanner squeezed her hand.

Whitney gave him a sympathetic look. "But she wasn't all that bighearted when she sent you out the door, blaming you for all the things she didn't like about herself."

He smiled at her. "I don't remember you doing that."

Could she ever say sorry enough? "Well, I do. That's what it boiled down to. I was finding a way out so I wouldn't have to face situations I wasn't comfortable in."

"We all dodge those."

"I know. But not everyone judges others with such broad strokes." She hated to admit that she had done that.

"You have good reason."

"Maybe but it's time to grow up and face my past and not automatically think the worst of people." It would still be hard for her in some social situations but now she was aware of her shortcomings so maybe she could make some changes.

"What brought on this reevaluation?" He sounded as if he really wanted to know.

"Would you believe that the most popular girl in my high school class came to me for help? It turns out the beautiful people of the world all have problems too. I realized after she left that I was the lucky one."

"Why?" Tanner turned and they headed back toward her house.

"Because my issues were ones that I could control. I just had to be willing to do it. I went back to my eating disorder class. I'm even going to become a facilitator. I want to help others through my experiences."

"That's great. I know you'll be good at that. You've certainly taught me a thing or two."

She looked at the handsome face she'd missed so much. "Have I, now? I can't imagine me teaching you anything."

Tanner stopped and brought her into his arms. "You've done something no one else could do."

"What's that?"

"Shown me how to love and be loved." He kissed her gently.

"Do you really love me?"

Tanner grinned. "Did you hear me say it?"

"I did, but I'd like to hear it again."

"I love you, Whitney." She had no doubt he meant it.

"And I love you with all my heart."

Tanner pulled her close. "That's more than I've ever deserved. Now, if you don't mind I'd like to go back to your house and show you just how much I love you."

Whitney rested her head against his chest. "I can't think of anything that I would like more."

EPILOGUE

IT HAD BEEN nothing but blue sky and sunshine at the Garonne Winery and Château. Whitney couldn't have asked for a more perfect wedding day. She had walked between two rows of grapevines to where Tanner stood on the exact spot where they had shared their first real kiss.

They had chosen to share their own vows. Tanner's were so full of love that Whitney hurt with the poignancy of them. For a man who'd said he knew nothing about love, he was a quick study. Once he'd learned to feel and say the words, he never stopped.

She was surrounded by her family and friends, all smiling and enjoying a good time in the cellar of the winery where the reception was being held. Marie and Malcolm had insisted on taking care of the wedding details when she and Tanner had told them they wished to marry at the winery. Marie had tastefully taken Whitney's wishes and created a day to remember.

To both her surprise and Tanner's as well, his parents attended. There was a tenseness to their meeting but otherwise there was nothing but blessings for the bride and groom. Tanner had asked his brother, Mark, to be best man and he had accepted. They had grown closer during the weeks before the wedding. For that, Whitney was grateful.

"What's the bride doing over here by herself?" Mr. Wilcox asked.

"Just thinking about how happy I am."

The band started up a new tune.

"May I have this dance, Mrs. Locke?" Mr. Wilcox made a slight bow her direction.

She liked the sound of her new name. "I'd be honored."

He led her in a box step around the open area surrounded by tables. "I told you I would be dancing at your wedding."

Whitney smiled. "You did but I didn't believe it."

They made one more turn before Tanner tapped Mr. Wilcox on the shoulder. "Mind if I break in? I'd like to dance with my beautiful wife."

Mr. Wilcox gave her hand to Tanner and kissed her on the cheek. "Life and love are fragile things. Treasure them. Not all of us get a second chance."

"So I have learned." Tanner looked into her eyes. "Now that I recognize it, and have it, I'm never going to let it go."

* * * * *

If you enjoyed this story, check out these other great reads from Susan Carlisle

**THE DOCTOR'S SLEIGH BELL PROPOSAL
WHITE WEDDING FOR A SOUTHERN BELLE
MARRIED FOR THE BOSS'S BABY
ONE NIGHT BEFORE CHRISTMAS**

All available now!